# Slipping
# the
# Moorings

# Slipping the Moorings

*Stories*

Susan McCallum-Smith

ENTASIS PRESS

WASHINGTON, D.C.

Published by
ENTASIS PRESS
Washington, D.C.
2008

ISBN 978-0-9800999-2-8

Library of Congress Control Number: 2008905015
Publisher: Entasis Press
Washington, D.C.

*The Housekeeper* first appeared in another form in *The Baltimore Review*.

Quotes from *The Sheik* in *Day of the Dead* reprinted by permission of Paramount Pictures Corporation.

Cover painting, *Island Life,* by Louis Sinclair McNally, 2008.

*With gratitude to the many wordsmiths who guided me through this collection, in particular the "little group of serious writers," and to Ed, for keeping the faith.*

*For Mum, Billie, David, and Meg.*

*And for Arthur, always.*

# Contents

# Slipping
# the
# Moorings

# Ploughman's Lunch

"YOU HAVEN'T CHANGED ONE BIT," she says after he finishes reading his list to her in the pub.

"Give me a chance, Nancy—it's only been four weeks."

But she doesn't give him a chance. She ups and leaves, her prawn cocktail barely touched, his steak and kidney pie still steaming. Shaken, Tom pulls a twenty-pound note from his wallet and tucks it under his pint of Tetley's bitter. That should cover it. By the time he gets to the door, she's scarpered.

Tom can't tell which way she's gone. Hampstead, an unfamiliar neighborhood. A bit fancy. She chose the pub, of course, but he'd have met her wherever she wanted. If it were East Finchley, he'd know where to look. He'd look near the bus stop (numbers 29, 43, and 65A), or in Budgens, the grocers, or maybe outside the bookies where she'd often waited while he'd nipped in to put on a line. Or perhaps in the park by the Tube station, with its spattered ironwork railing, balding grass, carpet of pigeons— the familiar landscape where they'd spent almost half a century, just a few miles east of where he stands now, but a different setting, a different backdrop altogether.

The weather had lifted while they were inside, fiddling with the stiff menus, scanning the vegetarian entrees, the Euro cuisine, looking for something they recognized, avoiding each other's knees under the small table.

"Sorry," he'd said when he'd accidentally nudged her. She'd tugged at the hem of her dress, tucked her ankles beneath the settle. As if he'd see something he'd never seen before, as if they'd not been married for donkeys' years.

The high street is water-colored and blurry following the morning's downpour, its rooflines and brickwork smudged by the sun. Tom's heart thumps beneath his heavy tweed jacket. Taking his handkerchief from his breast pocket, he dabs his forehead as though this gesture alone might save the circumstances, then refolds it so as to hide its poor laundering. He replaces it over his heart with a pat and hears the list he wrote for Nancy crackle under his palm.

His knees click and rattle beneath his Sunday-best trousers. He should find somewhere to plonk himself down. A telephone box stands across the street. Perhaps, he thinks, he should ring his daughter. Janice always knows how to handle her mother.

He steps into the road, then hesitates. His wife is staying with Janice. She's only just told him. When he asked her in the pub why she was choosing to leave him after so many years, she said it was because at last she'd somewhere to go. Janice needed her since she got divorced. Needed her to be an unpaid nanny for those kids, more like.

Still, he can't very well telephone now. It would look like he's chasing her. "Stalking" the newspapers call it.

Tom steps back and stumbles against the curb, leans forward to steady himself. A taxi making a sudden u-turn almost clips him. Its brakes squeal.

"Hey, watch yourself!"

Someone grabs his arm, then releases it. Back on the safety of the pavement, he feels his heart punch against the wall of his chest. A sit-down, that's what he needs. Breathing space. His Janice. His girl. Traitor. Not a girl any more though: a grown woman of forty-three, still fuming over that pillock ex-husband of hers. And angry women stick together, don't they? It's natural that Janice would pick Nancy's team, not his.

The shops and businesses on Hampstead's high street shrink into the distance before him: boutiques with foreign-sounding names, hyphenated real estate agencies, twin signs painted dark green with gold lettering like the smart liveries of the Pullman coaches he once took from Paddington to Brighton. Bric-a-brac fills the window of an antique dealer. Other people's musty leavings. Why would anyone buy such tat?

Across the road, a sandwich board advertising an exhibition props open an art gallery door. He can't read it from here, too fuzzy. Can't return to the pub neither— too embarrassed about his clumsy departure. Imagine Nancy having a prawn cocktail! She always had a ploughman's lunch in their local. He'd ordered it for her automatically when the waitress came over from behind the bar.

"Excuse me, Tom," Nancy had said, placing her hand on his arm while he was mid-sentence (the only time she'd touched him, besides letting him kiss her "hello," her cheek floury with powder, the scent of Steradent and clean cotton), "I think I'm quite capable of choosing what I want."

A glass of water, too, would go down a treat. Tom pulls the handkerchief from his pocket again. What will he do if she doesn't come back? Swiping under both eyes, the taste of salt on his lips, he makes for the pedestrian crossing. He concentrates on controlling his breathing, marching as he'd done during drills in the National Service. The pills in his trouser pocket will do the trick if his trouble returns. Nancy always looked after his pills. He doesn't know where she kept his prescription, or what will happen when these run out. In all the fuss, he's forgotten to ask her.

Think about it later. Right, left. Right. Left.

A table just inside the gallery holds empty champagne glasses bruised by lipstick, a dish of peanut shells, and a pile of glossy catalogues. Tom leans against it, rumpling a cloth crunchy with salt. His fingers brush the catalogues and he picks one up, folds it in half long-ways and puts it in his pocket.

He collects catalogues. Done it for years. Keeps them, too. It's not so much the stuff in them that he likes, as much as their wholeness, their brevity. He doesn't have his reading glasses, though. After the news on the telly tonight, he'll give it a glance.

There are no chairs here. Nowhere to rest. Beyond a staircase, he passes through double doors into an exhibition hall, receiving a welcoming slap of air conditioning. Large paintings hang on all sides; people mill before them like travelers in a railway station straining at timetables. In the center is a rectangular leather stool, toffee-colored and vacant. Tom shuffles over and sits down, the catalogue rising from his pocket to poke him in the chest. He sticks it under his thigh for safekeeping.

That's better. He draws breath and closes his eyes. He tries to remember how Nancy looked, sitting in the dusky air of the pub. Red and green droplets of refracted light from its stained-glass windows had drifted over her cream silk blouse. But no, he frowns, the blouse is wrong. It's a different blouse he sees. *Broderie anglaise,* they used to call it. Brilliant white cotton punctured like a cake doily, unbuttoned to her waist, and underneath, bare skin sprinkled with freckles, the pale breasts hidden, flattening toward the grass. She lies against the lush green of Hampstead Heath, thick copper tendrils of her hair licking the blades. High summer singes the back of his neck. She laughs and arches her spine. Oh, he is on fire. A memory unbidden after so many years.

"You're like me," a voice says. Someone sits beside him. The stool hisses, and Tom tilts into the speaker like a survivor in a lifeboat. He inches sideways, opening his eyes.

"When I arrive at an exhibition, I always pause for a moment before deciding where to begin." The clipped, public-school voice belongs to a young man with a light brown face. Pakistani, Indian, tanned, Tom can't tell. Everyone's such a mixture these days. Half the time he doesn't know what anyone is. He lifts a hand to his heart, which continues to pound, though with less ferocity. Nancy at nineteen years old. Who'd have thought it? A firecracker, a corker, a Rita Hayworth.

The young man crosses one leg over the other. "So many people," he murmurs. "Who'd have thought?"

"It's hot out," says Tom, sharper than he meant. He doesn't want to be stuck with a talker. Not today.

"True." The young man chuckles. "You're probably right—it's the air conditioning, not the art, that's packing them in." He looks as if he may add something else, but says instead, "Would you like some water?"

"Yes, yes, I would." The young man stands up and walks away. "Thank you," Tom adds.

Too late, the young man's out of earshot, heading into an adjoining gallery. Elegant from the back, in his dark trousers, black t-shirt, and shiny black belt and shoes. He looks like a hairdresser from one of those fancy modern salons. The kind of place Tom's daughter likes, where they charge thrice as much for a short back and sides as a barber, and cut it squint.

His eyes close. Yes, Nancy's still there, arched against the grass. One knee bent and up, her hands tucked behind her head like a girl painted on the side of a bomber. She winks.

Now the young man is standing before him, offering a glass of water and a napkin. The water fizzes, heavy with ice. A wedge of lime bobs on top. The young man hands over the glass before sinking down beside him again. The stool heaves and settles; then they both stare straight ahead, looking for shore. Tom sips the water. It tastes like Alka-Seltzer. He nods as people approach, but they tend to glance away from him and his companion before swerving around the stool as if it's a dead cat on a road. Every time the doors swing open, the young man turns to see who enters.

"I'm waiting for someone," he says.

"I gathered that."

Not that Nancy is a redhead now. Her color and curls fizzled out over the years. She's had a haircut since Tom last saw her. He remembers how different it looked in the pub, what with all the permanent gone.

"You've had your hair done," he'd said.

"Yes." She raised a hand to her neck.

"Looks nice." He hadn't liked it, too short and spiky. When she comes to her senses and returns home, he'll drop a hint.

"I'm going back next week to get it colored," Nancy said. "Red."

"Are you daft, woman?"

"You liked it well enough when we were young."

"Yes, but that was *then*, Nancy, and this is now. You're no spring chicken, you know. You don't want to look like mutton dressed as lamb."

"Is it a whole barnyard of insults you're planning, Tom, or just the two?"

He smiles. That was vintage Nancy. Sharp as flint. Still, her haircut had been recent, maybe even that very morning. A woman doesn't go to all the expense of a set and blow-dry just to tell her husband to get lost, does she?

"That's a good sign," he says.

"What is?" The young man looks up. A group of visitors stand in front of the large canvas filling the main wall. A woman with an earring in her nose shakes her head. Another woman taps a catalogue against her thigh, sighs, and moves on.

"Her hair-do."

"Oh." His companion glances over his shoulder. More visitors enter. "People taking care of themselves is always a good sign," he says. He holds out his hand. "Sean."

"Jenkins. Tom Jenkins." Tom hadn't pegged the young man as a Sean. He tries not to let his surprise show as he shakes Sean's hand. He wants to do his best to keep up with the times. Not keeping up with the times is one of his faults, according to Nancy. Sean—just the one name, then. That too, Tom knows, is fashionable.

He sits up straight and tries to pay more attention. Now that they're introduced, he feels politeness is required of him. Nancy was always shy with strangers, and Tom liked to show her how it's done.

Sean's gaze scours the room, as if he were poised on the brink of questions, holding himself back. Tom tries to think of something to say to break the ice.

"Isn't it funny," he says, "how everyone seems to be going around in a clockwise direction?" He sips his water. The lime wedge bumps against his teeth.

"Yes," Sean says, "I've noticed that, too." He stares intently at a woman by a canvas in the corner. She scribbles notes in a small brown book. Sean turns to Tom. "Do you collect art, Mr. Jenkins?"

"Oh, no." Tom prods the lime aside with a finger, but it drifts back like persistent flotsam. "I've had no time for that kind of stuff, and it'd take me too long to choose what to buy." They couldn't afford it, that's a fact, not that he'd admit it to all and sundry. He takes the lime from the glass and rolls it in the napkin. "After I retired, the wife and I spent time doing stuff to the house, but more do-it-yourself than anything." He smiles. "More plumbing than pictures." After considering the napkin for a moment, he sticks it in the pocket of his trousers. "But my wife, on the other hand, she'd like to collect."

"Really?" Sean straightens his spine. "What would she collect?"

"Well," Tom hesitates. What makes him think about those ditsy ideas she used to have? About taking a pottery class or trying her hand at poetry, or learning how to do those brass-rubbings in churches. Game, was Nancy. Always saying: *I fancy giving that a go, Tom.* She flitted from daft idea to dafter, never settling, prattling on when they first got married, but what with him losing his job for a while and her needing to work, none of it had seemed practical, and he'd put his foot down. Mind you, it had taken a few years to set her straight.

"I don't know," he says. "I don't know what she'd collect."

"What would she say about that one over there?" Sean points at the bright purple canvas that had fascinated the scribbling woman a moment earlier. Tom looks at the painting properly for the first time since entering the gallery. It doesn't seem to be a picture of anything, just a row of stripes in darkening tones of the same shade.

"Well, she'd like the color, right off."

"She wouldn't find it difficult?"

"Find what difficult?"

"The color."

"Are colors difficult?"

"My God, yes." Sean leans back on the stool, balancing his weight with his arms. Tom glances sideways. The young man must be a hairdresser after all.

"Not to my wife," says Tom. "She can be very difficult about a lot of things, but not colors." He touches his tie. He chose this combination of yellow and brown stripes with the yellow handkerchief for their lunch date, remembering that Nancy mentioned in the past that it matched nicely with his best sports jacket. Yet she hadn't said how smart he looked.

"Is she here?"

"Who?"

"Your wife?"

"No, no, she's not."

"And what do you think?"

"I don't know what to think, she's never done anything like this before." The room is suddenly claustrophobic. Bottoms jiggle before him—in denim, flowery silk, gabardine. "Not in all the years I've known her." Tom places the glass on the floor between his feet, and fishes a pill out from his trouser pocket, bumping Sean with his elbow.

"Sorry, son," he says.

"What for, Mr. Jenkins?"

He'll just take one. For his angina, for the shock. He picks up the glass, drinks, swallows. He'd apologized to Nancy in the pub, too. And she never told him exactly what he'd done wrong, acting like he should know. So he apologized for everything, thinking that way he'd be sure.

"She's an artist, then?"

"Who?"

"Mrs. Jenkins."

"Yes. No. Not really. She tried those painting-by-number things for a while, but she wasn't any good at it and —I'll be frank—I don't see any point in plugging away at something you'll never be good at. Life is long and hard enough without additional disappointments. Keep your head down and get on with it, that's my motto."

Sean doesn't appear to be listening. He has swiveled around on the stool to face the gallery doors. A young woman enters, holding a mobile phone and a pile of catalogues. She talks to two men in cream linen suits carrying champagne glasses. Tom considers their impractically small rectangular-framed glasses and their too-long sideburns. The woman pauses and looks at Sean before gesturing him to join her. Sean frowns and rapidly shakes his head. She turns away.

"Is that who you're waiting for?" says Tom, relieved. He'd been beginning to fear this Sean bloke might be a fairy.

"Not really."

"Very pretty." The girl is wearing a red dress. Nancy wore a red dress the night she told him she was expecting. Her hair all puffed up high—the late fifties that would have been. Thrilled to bits, he was. They were ready to go out somewhere, a work social or a Christmas dance most likely. She leaned against the kitchen sink with a glass of water in her hand.

"So that's that," she said. "Too late to do anything about

it now."

"What do you mean?" he said. "It's wonderful news — it's — it's the natural progression of things." He moved over to hug her, and she turned away and poured the rest of her water down the sink. Pulling the dress off her shoulders, he kissed along her hairline. (Nancy, Nancy with the bright red hair.) She hadn't protested, just looked out the window into the dark garden. The neighbors probably saw them. He couldn't have cared less.

But they'd only had Janice. Tom had quite fancied more, but it wasn't to be. He didn't know why, come to think of it; it wasn't something they talked about. After Janice's birth, the frolicking in the kitchen stopped. But that, too, is the natural progression of things. By the time he'd left off working at Bothwell's Machinery (factory equipment, pumps and motors) and started at Malkings & Company (farm equipment, threshers and motors), he was on nightshift. Months could go by without them being under the same blankets at the same time. Recently, what with his angina and her insomnia, they bought two single beds so's not to keep bumping into one another. (Bumping into Nancy, Nancy with the bright red hair.) She sat up half the night sewing. He slept face down.

"So, if Mrs. Jenkins doesn't paint, what does she like?"

Tom lifts his head sharply. What's this nosy bugger after?

"I'm being rather insensitive, aren't I? Asking you questions about your family when we've barely met."

Large print books from the library with covers of flushed semi-clothed women against a backdrop of mine shafts. BBC quality serials, the color lilac, Marks and Spencer's gift vouchers, tea from a cup not a mug. She likes to redecorate rooms, over and over. Wouldn't be so bad if only she'd stick to magnolia. Used to like designing and making clothes for herself and her friends. Fancied making a little business out of it, but he'd been afraid people would laugh at her, afraid she'd make a fool of herself. She told him he knew nothing about fashion but he'd been around spirit levels long enough to know a wonky hem when he saw one.

Huffs. She likes to go off in a huff and leave him to work out what's wrong. Traps and minefields. "Antsy Nancy" he'd called her. It had been gentle fun, a ribbing, not meant any harm, not meant to be taken as truth. After forty-five years of marriage, you'd think a woman would know you loved her, that she wouldn't need the telling.

"I don't know," Tom says. "I don't know what she likes."

Sean nods slowly. He's not really listening to me, Tom thinks. He looks so young. He can't be that much older than our Vicky.

"Our granddaughter's just got into Art College," he says. Nancy had told him in the pub, her face pinched, fingering the beer mat under her lemon and lime.

"Really? Which one?"

"Near Charing Cross Road, I think she said."

"St. Martins?"

"That's it."

"You must be pleased. It's very prestigious."

"I suppose so." Tom swirls the ice in his glass. "Wife's thrilled to bits." Nancy's mouth in a straight line. Red lipstick bleeding over the edges of her thin lips, waiting for his response to this news. Traps and minefields.

"But I'm still waiting to know what you think, Mr. Jenkins."

"About what?"

"The art."

Tom's opinions used to suffice for both him and Nancy. Now he's not so sure. Sean seems interested, however — insistent even. He'll do his best.

"If the Red Sea would just part, I'd take a look."

As if on command, the bodies in front of them shuffle aside and Tom has a clear view of a large canvas. Strips of masking tape bisect loud orange paint.

"Let's see now." Tom looks around for somewhere to

place his sweaty glass. He's pockmarked the bleached pine floor with it already. He jams his knees together, sticks it on his lap.

"I like things in a painting," he says. "Know what I mean? Recognizable things. Not still lifes, necessarily, especially those ones with the dead fish in them. I've never understood the attraction of that." He's quite chuffed with this beginning, with the sound of his own voice, and knowing that for the first time in many years he'll be able to make his point without being interrupted by Nancy's sighs.

"But landscapes, now, those I like. I like trees and somesuch, things I can recognize, a nice view that stays the same however often you go back to it."

Sean appears to expect more. His black eyebrows hang high on his forehead; his chin digs into his palm. For the second time that day, Tom senses someone wants a greater effort from him than he can muster. He looks again at the canvas in front him, with its vulgar splashy color and peeling stripes of what appears to be Elastoplast.

"Frankly, I think it's a load of pretentious tripe."

Sean presses his palms together as though in prayer. He whistles softly through his fingers.

"You painted all these, didn't you?" The revelation is sudden but unquestionable. How could he have been so daft? If Nancy had been here, she'd have guessed it right off. She'd have nudged him before he'd made such a plonker of himself. "You've got to realize, son," he rushes to amend, "I know nothing about art."

"Some would say neither do I."

The woman in the red dress appears at Sean's elbow.

"Here's your young lady now!" Tom says, rather loudly, grateful for the interruption.

The woman gives him a school-marm-ish glance, while tapping Sean's arm.

"Are you OK?" she says.

"Sure!" Sean sits up straight. "Amelia, this is Mr.

Jenkins. Mr. Jenkins, this is, unfortunately not my young lady, but Amelia, a colleague of mine."

Amelia nods at Tom. He brushes his right hand against his trousers to remove any dampness from the glass, but she's no longer paying him any attention.

"They love it," she whispers to Sean. "They really do. Absolutely fantastic."

"I'm not blind, Amelia."

She reads from her notebook. "Fresh and daring. Innovative. Dangerous."

"Bullshit."

"I think they're smashing," says Tom. "Smashing."

"Why, thank you, Mr. J."

"Don't jump to conclusions, Sean," says Amelia.

"Have my parents called?" Sean asks. She shakes her head. "They're not coming, are they?"

"It's early yet, and you know how absolutely murderous it is trying to park around here."

"I'd rather they didn't. Not if it's going to be panned."

"Would you like me to call them?"

"God, no."

Amelia sighs, straightens up and smoothes the front of her smooth red dress. Tom feels as if he were eavesdropping on someone's private business. He should get going. He tries to stand but the sticky toffee stool defeats him. The room feels odd again, not claustrophobic this time, but quieter than before. It's another of my turns, he thinks, but then he sees he's not the only one to notice. The people beside him pause, alert. Sean cocks his head.

"That's funny," he says.

A noise, of which Tom had only been half-aware, has stopped. Amelia's eyes widen, then she bolts, like a disturbed hare, to one corner of the gallery. She lifts one elegant arm and waves it under a ceiling vent, like a spectator under a hot air balloon. Tom lifts his hand, momentarily tempted to wave back.

"Christ," she hisses, scurrying over. "The air

conditioning's died." She flips open her phone.

"Fantastic," Sean says. "Tragedy to farce."

"Don't worry."

"Who's worried?" Sean lifts a glass of champagne from a passing tray.

"Don't worry," Amelia repeats, biting her lip. "I'll get the gallery director. Christ, where will we find an air conditioning engineer on a weekend?"

"I doubt it's that, pet," Tom says. "Most likely, it's just a fuse." Amelia looks at Tom as if she's never seen him before.

"A fuse," Amelia says. "What does that mean? Is it better or worse?"

"I don't know, but..."

"Would you know one, if you saw one?"

Tom laughs. "Of course, pet, are you daft? I used to..."

She reaches down and suddenly he's on his feet. She links one arm through his and they quick-step through the gallery doors. He'd be enjoying it if they weren't rattling along so fast.

"Hey, me too," says Sean. Tom turns and sees the young man following behind them holding his champagne glass.

Outside in the empty hall, Amelia releases Tom then strides around nudging doorways open with her elbows, while fiddling with her phone.

"Bet your biscuits, it's in a little cubby hole," Tom says, leaning against the banister, catching his breath. He notices a doorway under the large staircase and walks over to pull it open. He tugs at a piece of string attached to a bulb and, sure enough, when the light comes on, he sees a battered metal fuse-box mounted on the wall in the far corner.

"Knew it," Tom says.

"Look at that, Ame," says Sean. "He's like a homing pigeon."

Amelia squeezes behind them into the tiny room under the stairs and they bundle up together like lemmings before the fuse box. Tom opens its door while Amelia breathes over his shoulder. She smells exotic, like Indian food, a bit spicy but nice. Not like Nancy though, Nancy always smells like clean laundry.

"How do you know which one it is?" she asks. "Will you have to take them all out? How do you repair them? Can you repair them? Or do you have to get another one? What's that thingy for? That dangly thingy. That's not supposed to dangle like that, is it? Is that what's gone wrong?"

"Listen, pet, why don't you go back to ..." He has no idea what she does. "Go back to ..."

"Peddling tripe," Sean says.

"I do not peddle tripe!"

"I know, Ame, I know," Sean says. "Off you go anyway," he kisses her cheek. "This is man's work." He shuts the door behind her.

Tom strains to read the faded pencil marks labeling the fuses while Sean pokes around.

"Isn't this cozy?" Sean says. Folding chairs are stacked against one wall. A security guard's hat hangs on a hook above a wooden stool next to pallets of bottled water. On top of the stool are copies of *The Sun,* and an ashtray full of cigarette butts under a disconnected smoke detector.

"We need a spare," Tom says. He runs his hand over the top of the box and into the cobwebbed nooks and crannies beyond. He feels too hot, but it's good to have something to do. He takes his jacket off then looks for somewhere to put it, forgetting for the moment his shirt's un-ironed back and sleeves and the soggy stain on his trouser pocket from the napkin.

"I'll hold it for you," Sean says, taking it from him.

"Thanks, son."

Sean reads the inside label. "Classy," he says. He shrugs it over his shoulders and puts it on, running his fingers down its lapels.

"Aha! Found one." Tom pulls a fuse from a shoebox

wedged down the side of a generator. "Now let's see..."

Sean peeps out the door, then shuts it sharply. "Lord, don't want to meet *them*."

"Come on," Tom mutters. The old fuse is stubborn, adamant that it's not for turning. "Shift come on, come on... gotcha, you bugger!" He hands the broken fuse to Sean, who takes it gingerly, then puts it on a shelf. Tom plugs the new fuse in, and asks Sean to check. Sean sticks his head out the door again.

"Yep," he says, "It's back on."

Tom examines the other fuses wondering if he should twiddle with any more, reluctant to close the box. He's done everything he can, though, so he doesn't, and turns around.

"Wait," Sean says. "Let's not go yet." He opens one of the folding chairs and sits down. Tom hesitates, then moves the newspapers and perches against the stool.

"This reminds me of the janitor's office at my old prep school," Sean says.

"Our janny had one too."

"He used to have a bucket..."

"...with sand in it," completes Tom.

"Yes!" Sean says.

"For when the kids threw up," says Tom. "Or blood from fights or falling over. Nothing changes, son."

Still, it's not his school janitor's cubby that Tom sees; it's his father-in-law's hall cupboard decades ago. Nancy and he had been stepping out for a while, but her father was old-fashioned and insisted they were never to be alone together in the house. Tom had sneaked by one morning after her father had gone to work. He'd been hovering on the brink of a momentous threshold, struggling with Cross-Your-Heart's most complicated bra-strap single-handed, when they heard the front door slam. They bolted off the living-room sofa and into the hall, where Nancy yanked him inside the cupboard under the stairs just as her father rounded the bend heading for the kitchen.

She told him to shoosh. Inside the cupboard was coal-mine black. Tom couldn't see her, but he sensed her. Every fiber of his body trembled so much he was frightened he'd joggle the ironing board pressed against his spine. He closed his eyes and matched his breathing with hers (breathing with Nancy, Nancy with the bright red hair). He was blind yet electrified; she was all around him, like water, like current. He heard her father mutter to himself as he walked back down the hallway. The letterbox rattled. Taking the newspaper out, most likely. The front door creaked open then slammed shut. The garden gate clanged. Tom sensed Nancy inch forward, until her eye rested on the chink of light in the door jamb, until he saw one stray curl flare and glint like copper wire.

He doesn't mind the new haircut anymore. He wouldn't care if she dyed it red.

Tom looks at the young lad opposite him. Sean sits like a footballer who's been red-carded, his head hanging down, swinging the empty champagne glass between his legs, dwarfed by the oversized, old-fashioned tweed jacket, staring at the floor between his feet, hen-toed in their shiny black shoes.

"You can't hide in here forever, son," Tom says.

The door is yanked open, filling the small space with light and cool air.

"What on *earth* are you doing?" says Amelia. "Everyone's looking for you."

"We're saving the day. Or I should say, Mr. J. is saving the day."

"You should be mingling!"

"I *am* mingling. I'm mingling with Mr. J."

"Oh, don't worry about me," says Tom. "I don't need looking after."

"We fixed it," says Sean.
"I know. The air conditioning man's here. And an electrician."

Not the thanking kind, then, this Amelia. Two men

stand behind her, looking impatient and annoyed. What a load of palaver, Tom thinks, over a blown fuse. Sean hasn't moved.

Amelia points toward the gallery. "Out," she says, "now."

"We've had our marching orders," Sean says.

He goes, wearing Tom's jacket. Tom follows him, leaving Amelia and her engineers to tussle into the cubby under the stairs.

"Nice girl, though," says Tom. "Bright." Sean nods. "If I were you, I'd be tempted to ask her out her out for a spot of something." Sean doesn't reply. "A bit of dinner, or an ice-cream in the park."

Tom returns to the empty stool—the abandoned catalogue, like a traffic cone, having somehow saved his parking spot—and plops himself down. Sean slips off the jacket and lays it over Tom's knees. He smiles with the resigned expression of a school boy caught out in a prank. Tom feels that way too. Sean begins a reluctant mingling, pausing to talk to visitors who look, to Tom, as if they'd really rather he didn't.

Tom's old water glass still sits on the floor. He picks it up then replaces it. He looks at the floorboards, at the smudged concentric rings.

The housekeeping had been more than he'd expected. It didn't fall into untidiness slowly; it happened all at once, in a rush. Dishes in the kitchen sink unwashed from the night before. Burnt cheese stuck to the grill. Sideboard drawers jammed with pension books and unpaid bills. The washing machine, the iron, the microwave, hesitating with his hand shaking over the sugar bowl, unsure about how many spoons to put in his tea, to get it the way he liked it.

He told her that over lunch at the pub, all the things he'd learned in four weeks, all the little kindnesses he'd uncovered. He'd written the list and ticked the items off as he read to her, not wanting to forget any of them, afraid that the one he missed might be the one that started it all. Surely an apology this detailed would be enough?

"You never listened to me, Tom," she said. "I doubt you heard one word I uttered these past forty years."

"Forty-five years, Nancy. We've been married forty-five."

"Or looked at me, neither"

"Marriage is about going through life side by side, not face to face." He believes this to be true. Always has. If he'd glanced sideways, she'd be there. Never assumed it would be otherwise.

He regrets having said that now. He regrets ordering her the ploughman's lunch. Most of all, to be honest, he regrets the uneaten steak and kidney pie. In the past month he's lived off tinned soups. Filling up the small basket in Budgens with different Campbells varieties, ignoring the sniggers of that ugly teenager at the till whose skin was all cratered by acne.

And what a fuss she'd made when he suggested she cancel those artsy magazine subscriptions, or move her Singer sewing machine into the shed to make more space for when the grandkids came around. Such things shouldn't matter so much, and he told her so in the pub.

"See?" she said, triumphant. "That's exactly what I mean."

"Twenty-three days, fourteen hours and," he looked at his watch, "twenty-eight minutes—that's how long it's been since you left me, Nancy. You can't say now that I don't pay attention."

An elegant middle-aged Indian woman in a sari has paused in the gallery doorway. She holds the hand of an older man with ginger hair heavily striped with gray. The woman sees Sean, smiles, and holds her arms wide. Sean bounds over and kisses her on both cheeks before grasping the hand of the man. Tom turns back to the canvas in front of him. When did this happen? How had he not seen the landscape melting into orange blocks and masking tape?

And the sight of Nancy's slip had caused him to stutter and stumble. And she had lain back on Hampstead Heath and laughed and laughed, and her hair had unraveled like hanks of russet wool, rolling and tumbling over the grass.

Nancy and her lack of practicality. Nancy—how he'd reined her in, ironed her out, undone her, straightened her into something recognizable as a wife and mother.

Sean, the man, and the woman pass Tom on their way into an adjoining gallery, arms linked in a row, the youngest a perfect blend of the older two, like a well-stirred soup. Arms linked in a row they go, as Tom, Nancy, and Janice used to do every summer while strolling the pier at Brighton. Tom stands up stiffly. His best sports jacket slithers off his lap. The mashed catalogue falls to the floor. His foot clips the empty glass.

Outside, the afternoon light is harsh. He walks to the bench under the plastic shelter of the bus stop and sits down. This is Hampstead High Street, he thinks, those green signs exist, that black cab, this red bus trundling toward  him. He closes his eyes. There can be no argument against such clarity.

# High Rise

THE NIGHT BEFORE VISITING MALKY in prison, Allison dreams she flies out of the high rise. She is wee again, and getting ready for primary school, already dressed in her uniform. She steps over the shoebox of paper dolls cut from the *Bunty* comic, leaving behind the cup of hard-boiled egg mixed with butter on the arm of the sofa. She opens the door to her granny's veranda, a toty balcony tucked into the side of the block of flats, thirteen floors up, and the toastiness of the living room is replaced by a nippy autumn morning sawing at her face.

She's not supposed to go out on the veranda alone. The damp concrete is slidey under her socks. The daylight draws a pretend line splitting the floor between the shadowy puddled corners and the blinding sunshiny front. She grasps the metal railing with both hands, and swings one leg up and over, and then the other and perches on the ledge, balanced on her bum. She lifts a hand and looks at it; the palm is manky already and smells like the swing park. The wind blows up her gray school skirt and flaps the end of the tie that's tucked down her waistband and dangling between her legs.

She sits for a bit. The trees in Pollok Park are stirred together red and gold and orange. The milk floats clank in and out behind the Co-Op, and her pals dribble from the newsagents having spent their lunch money on crisps and sherbet dabs before heading to school. Posh violin music drifts up from the corporation depot where the buses go to sleep at night, next to the vandalized tennis courts in the park.

She shunts her bum off the edge of the veranda and lets go.

As she hurtles toward the ground, Allison struggles to wake up. If she doesn't manage it before she hits she'll die. Dreaming of being dead meant you were dead, her granny told her that. Her face plummets to meet the pavement; she can almost feel the scrape and splatter and imagine humungous scabs knitting up and down her front, but whoosh!

She swoops, high, high over the top of the high rise, and down its other side, brushing the tips of those red and gold and orange leaves all stirring together in the park, skirting the gravy-brown burn, and the Maxwell's prize-winning Highland cows that stop chewing and lift their marmalade heads to watch her. Her heart bounces from her toes up to her throat, then flip-flops to a stop in the middle of her chest. She floats above Glasgow on her back, the sun warming her face and making sparkly confetti shapes under her eyelids.


Malky lifts his chin and places the razor carefully under his jaw bone, then draws it slowly, deliberately, down his throat, trying to ignore the prison guard visible in the mirror. It's hard to get a decent shave with a slimy prick adjusting his balls behind you. Malky's fingers trace his jaw bone from left to right, methodically removing the rest of the foam.

The guard steps forward, and nudges him swiftly in the crook of the knee.

Malky's leg buckles. He swears, gets his balance back. Blood trickles over his chin.

Oh, sorry pal, says the guard. Did I dunt ye?

Malky puts the razor down and picks up some toilet

paper to blot the cut. The guard takes the razor and drops it in a plastic bag.

I'm no done yet, says Malky.

You'll do.

Malky turns back to the mirror and combs his hair. He tugs at the sleeves of his clean blue prison overalls. He pays Tam in laundry with fags to starch them for him, to give the seams that gallus pointy edge.

I need to make my call, he says.

Missing yer mammy?

The guard waits outside the transparent phone booth while Malky makes the one telephone call he's allowed per week. After hanging up, Malky rests his head against the plastic and shuts his eyes, only opening them when he senses another inmate accompanied by a guard shuffling up outside. The inmate looks a bit mental. As the guards chat, the inmate grips the phone booth and starts shoogling it and bawling. Malky can't make out what the nutter is saying, but if he had to guess it would be: Hurry the fuck up!

Allison takes two painkillers and washes them down with milky tea. Some wonky cosmic joke has aligned her periods with her monthly visits to Barlinnie. She's leaking away to nothing. She'll be hollow by the time Malky gets out, like an empty nest, all the best bits of her gone. The one time in the month she wants to look half-way decent and her skin mottles with plukes and the blonde drains from her hair. She feels wrung out like a chip wrapper. Her pal, Carol-Anne, says she should get a grip, take herself off to that new spa in Argyle Street. Says she's acting like a widow in mourning, when she's not even married, as if Malky was dead, rather than away working in the Bar-L, as the local saying goes. Allison's having none of it; she's not getting tarted up or the neighbors' will be asking who for, when her man's in the jail?

She gets herself ready in the same thirteenth floor high rise flat that appears in her dreams, passed on to her by the council when her granny died. Malky had promised to buy her a new house in Bearsden, but he never managed it before he was arrested.

Allison's sister comes round to wash the windows when they're needing done, because Allison is so afraid of heights she won't go within one foot of any of them, never even lifts the blinds. She's on the waiting list for a council house at ground level, but because she's no kids, Scotland will have won the World Cup by the time she gets it.

She plasters concealer over the bags under her eyes. Her tummy is swollen and taut like a balloon. She slaps on one of those sticky heating pads, then pings her knickers over it to keep it secure. Gordon arrives just as she's leaving, carrying his toolbox, to install the new taps in the bathroom.

Anything you want me to tell him, she says, pulling her gloves on, avoiding his eyes.

No. Well, say hello and that.

When the lift comes, there's a puddle in the corner. She stands well away from it. As likely to be rainwater as piss but you can't risk it. The doors are closing when someone yells, Hold on!

It's Sorry from down the corridor. At least, that's what everyone calls him; she's clueless about his real name.

Oh, sorry, hen, he says, as Allison holds the doors open. Didn't mean to keep you back.

Sorry pushes a nicked Co-op supermarket trolley ahead of him into the lift. The council has evicted him for failing to pay his rent, and he's moving his stuff to his boyfriend's flat. Plastic bags of clothes plug the bottom of the trolley, and he wraps his arms over a huge aquarium balanced on the top, empty of water but filled with pretend plants and a miniature Disney castle.

Sorry, Allison, I didn't mash yer toes, did I? He glances up at her, sideways. You look smashing, by the way. Visiting day, is it?

Thanks, aye.

I'm knackered, so I am.

You must be done by now.

Near enough.

Allison peers into the aquarium. Is Clooney in there? she says. I canny see him.

Aye, sorry about that. He's hiding. He hates moving house. He's that stressed but, I'll no get him to eat for days.

Is it no gerbils you feed snakes?

Sorry's eyes widen like an owl.

I just gie him chicken. He likes the Markies shredded stuff, with a bit of salt and Branston on it. And he's daft for tablet. I'm sorry to say that's why he's nay teeth left.

So, he's a gummy snake?

Like the sweeties, aye.

Carol-Anne had leant Allison her new black Burberry raincoat, and she knots its belt tightly before stepping into the wind tunnel between the flats. A gust snatches her brolly and she spins around and slams her shoulder against it to keep it upright, then staggers across the car-park in her best black stilettos, dodging the puddles and the boys in hoodie jerseys playing keepie-uppie with a deflated ball, oblivious to the teeming rain. Under a bus shelter tattooed with graffiti, Allison puts her brolly down, and pats her newly-washed and now ruined hair. Don't know why I bloody bother, she thinks. The number 23 will arrive in a tick, hiding inside the next convoy, as if the very buses get lonely, as if the very buses are feart to cross the city on their own.

On a wet day like today, the visitors' hall in the Victorian wing of Barlinnie Prison reminds Allison of the public swimming baths. The bottom third of the walls are tiled in the same peely-wally green, before switching over to a dirty white paint up to its arched roof, scrolled over with some fancy plasterwork she can barely see. The long windows are opaque so she can't pretend to look at the view when the conversation lags. It's just the M8 motorway out there, but, and she hears the cars whiz past. Must drive the inmates spare, she thinks, hearing people accelerating off someplace else. At the beginning of the visits everyone whispers, trying to keep their business private from the other eleven tables sharing the hall, then they end up yelling at one another because it's like the ceiling steals the voices—does a runner with them like a shoplifter.

The tiles sweat with damp. It's clammy inside and out and Allison feels clammy too, with the heating pad plonked against her stomach. It's only ten past three but it could be the middle of the night under these florescent lights, she's yon sleepy way she used to get at school during double-maths. She tugs her black skirt over her knees and crosses her legs. Her tights are mud-spattered and a ladder has started inside one shoe. She can feel the punctured nylon strangling her wee toe.

So, how's work? Malky says.

No bad. Carol-Anne's covering for me the day.

Speak up, hen, I canny hear you.

It's this room. Drives me nuts, Allison says. It's not Malky's fault the hall has the acoustics of a railway station, but she's all riled up inside.

It's like my sentences come out long-ways as normal, she says. And then get sucked up. It's a big Hoover in here, so it is.

She calms down and tries again. Work's same as usual.

Work's not the same as usual, but there's no point telling Malky that. As a cook in the local primary school, she used to take turns at serving the lunches, but now she stays in the back, not minding about having to do more of the heavy work—heaving great platters of lasagna and mince pie in and out of the big ovens and chiseling it into slices. She can't stand being around the kids anymore. The wee ones, the primary ones and twos scare her the most, the four-and-five-year-olds—if one gives her a funny look over his plate of corned beef and chips, she's frightened she'll snatch him and run, and keep running, to the high rise, to the airport, to Florida, the moon. She'll morph into one of they monsters you read about in the paper, who steal other women's weans, and everyone will think she's a sick perv, when her sickness is only the wanting.

A guard leans against a wall behind Allison with his eyes shut and his hands in his pockets. Another stands behind Malky by the door to the prisoners' wing, playing with a handheld computer toy.

It's the waiting I can't stand, says Allison.

You don't need to tell me about that, hen, says Malky.

I feel like it's too late. She didn't mean to bring it up again, but there, she's said it.

What do you mean?

You know what I mean, says Allison.

No, I don't. Malky crosses his arms. The guard standing behind him curses at his computer game and jiggles it a bit. I don't fucking get your fucking meaning at all.

No need to swear, says Allison. Every time I try and talk about anything important you start swearing at me.

Malky looks at the clock. 3:15. Have you seen Gordon, he says.

No.

Malky had told her to stop moaning about the state of the flat and pay someone to freshen it up. So, when the sink got blocked a couple of months back, she gave Malky's younger step-brother, a plumber, a call. While Gordon was there, she told him to take a look at the bathroom and give her a quote for replacing the tiles and the taps with something more modern.

She left him sitting on the closed toilet seat, adding up his sums on a scrap of yellow paper with a bookie's pencil, and went into the kitchen to put the kettle on. Arithmetic was obviously not Gordon's strong point, because the tea was poured, the paper read, and a fag lit by the time he joined her. He gave her the slip of yellow paper and went over to the sink.

So…she said, reading it. These would be the gold taps, then?

You buy cheap, you pay dear, he said, sounding like an old sweetie-wife. He dumped his tools on the floor. Have you been stuffing tattie peelings down this? he said, pointing at the sink.

No, she said. I've been pouring money. I'm made from it, didn't you know?

Aye, right, very funny.

He took a plunger from his tool bag and rammed it over the kitchen drain. He reminded her of Malky, that's what gave her the idea. Even though they were only half-brothers, something in Gordon's pipe-cleaner frame wound around her heart and threatened to yank it straight through her chest. He was about the same height as Malky. Compact—the height to look her straight in the eye standing up or lying down. In tackety-boots, jeans and a Rangers football jersey, he was none too clean, a bit clatty in that not unpleasant style of workies in general.

Or maybe it was his pumping away at that blocked drain with such dogged determination that gave her the idea. She suppressed a snort at the outrageousness of it. Gordon, the little engine that could. Could he? It crossed her mind that she'd need to think up a stormer of an excuse to tell Malky. Claiming a miracle because she glimpsed the Pope on the telly wouldn't quite cut it. If he wanted a wean like she did, but, how much could he mind?

Carol-Anne didn't know how Allison could stand it, going without sex for months on end. She was always trying to pair Allison off with some man or other, reminding her that Malky was behind a locked door and a quick shot on the swings does wonders for a girl's complexion. If I was you, I'd be that horny, Carol-Anne said. I swear I'd be standing outside the post office offering to hump any randy old git going in to collect his pension, even the ones with missing legs and nae teeth.

Allison didn't miss sex, she missed sex with Malky. Since his arrest, her body had become dormant, like a wee animal; desire had curled in on itself, smothered its own flames and slept, its heart-beat tamped down to a murmur. She made an effort, but a lackluster one—still plucked her eyebrows but never bothered shaving her legs, the hair was soft on her shins now, like a pelt, and she hadn't bought new underwear for almost three years. She went to bed earlier and earlier every night, reading historical books from the library, watching the telly till she dozed, then dreamed of flying and falling. This is what it must be like to be old, she thought. To not really know if you're a man or a woman. Sometimes her own breasts surprised her. It was only around kids that something stirred, stretching in its sleep.

Stories of Malky's violence had reached her in roundabout ways, not long after she started going out with him. These didn't seem true, but, airy-fairy as Chinese whispers or the foreign news, because he'd only ever shown her a tremendous tenderness. A stomping, walloping tenderness, as if he'd belted her hard with it and knocked her out, and that's what kept her faithful all this time.

Gordon?

He turned around and looked at her.

How old are you?

Why?

Just wondered.

I'm twenty-three. He went back to rogering the sink with the plunger and swearing.

Gordon?

What? He sounded exasperated now. He put the plunger down.

He looked so like him, and they might only need to do it the once. It wouldn't be cheating, more like substituting from the bench within the same team.

Could you do us a favor? She said.

Allison glances at the clock—3:30—she's desperate for a fag. She takes cigarettes and a plastic lighter from her bag. Smoking is not allowed in the visitor's hall, but everybody does it. They tried enforcing the ban for a while but that almost started a riot. The ability to light a cigarette seemed to ensure one half of the room didn't reach over the tables and throttle the other half.

Maybe I did see Gordon, she says. Can't remember.

What's he up to? Malky says.

How should I know? I'm no your brother's keeper.

He's OK, but?

Well, he's no in here for a start, so he must be doing something right.

Allison rustles in her bag again. She pulls out her diary and takes a photograph from between its pages.

Want to see a picture of Carol-Anne's boy?

The guard steps forward to see what she's doing.

Keep your knickers on torn-face, she says, showing him the photograph, then grimaces at Malky. That bampot thinks I'm Holly Golightly in here with the weather report.

She holds the photograph up for Malky to see. He slips his hands in his pockets.

See that, she says, pointing at the baby. I could eat him.

Another talking sausage with a face like a well-skelped arse.

Allison shakes her head and bites her lip. You didn't even look at it, she says.

Your pal fair churns them out.

She returns the photograph to her bag. I've been thinking, she says.

Does it hurt?

Fuck off.

Tut, tut. Language.

I was reading something in a magazine the other day, and I think it's about time you and I found ourselves.

Why? Are we lost?

Allison stands up. She wants to leave this clammy place right now.

Oh, sit down, for Christ's sake. You could still start a

fight in an empty house.

Allison sits down, and fiddles with the hem of her skirt. Two tables over a woman yelps like an injured dog. The man she's come to visit shakes his head, stands up and nods at a guard. The guard takes him back into the prisoner's wing, leaving his visitor bubbling into her hankie, wiping her eyes and nose, before bundling herself away.

You've yet to tell me the good news, says Malky.

Allison looks at him sharply. What good news?

Malky glances at the clock again. I missed your birthday, he says.

Missed three of my birthdays, you mean.

Thirty-eight. A mature woman. I do like to get my mitts on a mature woman.

Ancient woman, more like.

When I get out I'll buy you something nice. Would you like that?

Allison blows smoke into the air.

Don't you think you should give these up now? he says. Allison frowns at her cigarette, then at Malky.

A cat, he says. You always wanted a cat.

The council doesn't let you have cats in the high rise.

Give us a break, hen. I'm doing my best.

Aye, well.

Malky slams his palms down on the table. Allison jumps, startled. She drops her cigarette onto the floor, and stamps on it to put it out. The guard behind Malky looks up from his computer game and clears his throat.

Calm down son, he says. Yer giving your bird the heebies.

What did you expect me to do? Malky whispers. Wank in an Irn Bru bottle and stick it in the post?

Allison feels as if a lump of coal plugs her throat. A noise escapes her, a whimper. Malky thinks it's a laugh. He smiles, revealing his small, even, white teeth, and reaches across the table and takes her hands.

You're a sight for sore eyes, sweetheart, he says. Haven't

changed a bit.

Allison shakes her head.

Remember that day in Pollok Park? He says.

She smiles and looks away. What would the guards do if she clambered over the table right now, she thinks, in front of all these people and onto Malky's lap and took him inside her? Clung to him like a limpet on a rock at Rothesey, her arms and legs latched onto his spine. She feels torn and empty, like one of those poly bags you see tossed around by the wind, snagged on hedges, hooked on pylons, all ripped and holey.

We nearly buggered the suspension in the car, so we did, he says.

Malky glances at the Guards. He begins to sing, softly. *It's just a perfect day, I'm glad I spent it with you. Just a perfect day...*

*You keep me hanging on,* Allison joins in. *You just keep me hanging on.*

She sees the guards gander at each other over their heads, and knows the inmates and visitors next to them are pulling faces and snorting. She doesn't care—she and Malky used to sing all the time, everywhere—on buses, in nightclubs, pubs, lifts, restaurants, even at the back of the Odeon in Sauchiehall Street. Before he'd got seven years for aggravated assault, half their conversations came with tunes attached. Other folk's stares have no more effect on them than the weather. A glance from Malky always shuts them up, and it works this time, too. He slowly turns his head and surveys everyone around them, until their audience sticks their noses back in their own business.

So, how's life in the high rise?

Allison pulls her hands away. How d'you think?

If you need anything you know you've only got to ask Hugh.

Hugh. Aye, right.

Allison could never work out exactly what Hugh did

for Malky, except that it fell under the category of miscellaneous. A bit of this, a bit of that, a bit of the other, Malky said, when asked.

On the morning of her thirty-eighth birthday, her plan for Gordon had gone skee-whiff, gone off the rails faster than a reformed alcoholic inheriting a bar. She'd just told Gordon to take his mean mochat self out of her sight, when the doorbell rang. She was still in her dressing gown when she opened it, thinking Carol-Anne had turned up early, and there stood Hugh, in the same leather jacket she remembered him wearing to a Duran Duran concert years before, and his hockey haircut seeping gel.

Oh, she said. It's you.

Happy Birthday, sweetheart, Hugh said. He lugged what looked like a four-liter-vodka-carry-out in an upside-down brown paper bag. He pulled the bag off with a pansy flourish to reveal a Hallmark gift box streaming lilac and yellow ribbons.

Gordon came stomping up the hall behind Allison, and stopped at the door.

I'm away, then, he said, zipping up his donkey jacket. He brushed past her, nodded briefly at Hugh, and belted toward the lifts. Moving that fast, thought Allison, still boiling with rage and embarrassment, like he'd a firecracker up his arse.

Here's your hat, where's your hurry, she muttered at his retreating back.

Adolescent chicken pox had gifted Hugh a face like a dartboard, and this ugly mug was now a stew of questions.

He's fixing my plumbing, Allison said. Did Malky send you over with this? She fingered the streamers, thinking her morning had perked right up.

Eh, no. No, this is from me.

Allison folded her arms. She swithered about what to do next, sniffing trouble in Hugh's generous sloshing of Old Spice.

Her next door neighbor's door opened. Mrs. McFadden's beady eyes followed her nose round the corner.

Oh sorry, pet, she said. I thought that was someone at my door.

Hugh glanced at her, then back at Allison. Mrs. McFadden had taken root.

Any chance of a nice cuppa? he said.

I guess you'd better come in, said Allison. And give me that, you look like a twat.

Thanks very much, sweetheart. Appreciate it. I'll no be a minute.

Allison headed for the kitchen, trailing lilac and yellow ribbons, leaving Hugh to shut the door behind him. Words ran out of him like a leaky dictionary, all down the hall, and onto the kitchen table, and through the boiling of the kettle, words about his mother, and his ex-wife, and those kids of his that were out of hand, and how lonely he was, and here she was, and Malky said he was to look after her, make sure all her needs were met, and it's her birthday, and did she never get lonely, sweetheart, and who would ever know?

Five minutes later Hugh was out in the corridor again with her handprint on his face and that nice cuppa inches from scalding his balls. Not that Allison would ever tell Malky about Hugh's amateur tackling of her tits in the kitchen, he'd lunged at her with his eyes shut and paws up like a blind goalie. Hugh might be a dingbat, but he didn't deserve to end up trussed in a rug at the bottom of the Clyde.


The rain has changed direction. Instead of falling down, it's driving along the M8 from Carlisle to Glasgow, needling at the windows as it passes Barlinnie.

Don't know why you don't marry that clock, Allison says, following Malky's glance. You're smitten with it, the day.

Thought I told you to get the flat fixed up.

I did, she says, managing to follow this sudden swerve

in the conversation.

And?

Jimmy papered the living room.

And?

And what?

Don't stop now, hen, spit it out.

Gordon's changing the tiles and the taps in the bathroom.

So you have seen him, after all?


Allison bought an ovulation test from Boots the chemist in town, though she didn't need it, she knew exactly when to ask Gordon to makes himself useful—on her birthday. He arrived early that Sunday morning. She'd been up half the night worried near to death and was still in her bathrobe. Didn't seem any point getting dressed only to take everything off again. She'd considered having a shower, shaving her legs, putting on a bit of make-up but that would have implied that this was something other than a favor, and the truth was, she was beginning to change her mind.

Out of most of the lassies she'd gone to school with, she was the only one who hadn't got pregnant in her teens or early twenties. Little Miss Smarty-pants had determined not to be shackled to a dunderhead and weans while barely an adult, and had taken herself to Dr. Matthews when she turned fifteen. I'll say this for the pill, she thought, it works, right enough.

She slipped her knickers off under her nightdress and lay down on top of her bed. She stared at the ceiling to avoid seeing Gordon get undressed. She heard him kick the tackety boots on the floor then unzip his jeans. Her heart hammered against her chest like someone trying to get out a burning house. If the wean looks a lot like Malky, she thought, maybe he won't mind so much. She risked a glance at Gordon, but Gordon's resemblance to Malky had fallen away with his clothes to the floor. He looked bigger, more muscled, and hard like a bully. His body was in better nick than Malky's, too, the age difference of almost twenty years showed. Suddenly, she felt horrified, horrified at the depth of her wanting and what she seemed prepared to do to feed it, and scared witless of Malky and what he'd say when he found out. And scared, too, of Gordon, scared of him hurting her, or worse, scared of him making her feel good. Oh my God, she thought, what if I can't help myself and I make a wee noise?

It's fucking freezing in here, Gordon said. Is the heating on?

She nodded.

What you doing on top of the bed? I'm going under the blankets. Are you coming with me? he said, or am I doing this on my own?

She jackknifed her legs up and scooted under beside him.

Jesus Christ, he said. When was the last time you shaved your legs? It'll be like shagging my dog.

He rolled over on top of her and scissored her knees apart with his own.

By the way, he said, This isn't a freebie.

You're kidding? She squirmed and lifted her head to look him straight in the eye.

She couldn't believe it, how he'd waited till her gingham nightie was scrunched around her waist before he mentioned money. Her body, already tense from top to toe, went as rigid as a plank of wood. Any minute now, she thought, he's going to be huffing away like a paratrooper doing press-ups, hammering her to the bed like a nail, and she knew she wouldn't be able to bear it.

Are you planning to lie there like a fucking doughnut? he said. Or are you gonny gie a boy a bit of encouragement?

That did it. It took all her self-control not to start wailing like a banshee on fire. She shoved him off and stumbled sideways, landing on her knees on the floor.

I've changed my mind, she said, pulling her nightdress

down.

Fucking typical, Gordon muttered. He got out of bed and started yanking his clothes back on, swearing under his breath. Women, he said. Would have been as much fun as a wake, anyways. Allison folded her arms and watched him, trying to maintain some self-control, roiling with embarrassment, knowing she had a brass neck and wishing he'd hurry up and get his bloody knickers back on and bugger off.

Not even a thanks for coming, he said, when he was fully dressed.

Aye, but you didn't, did ye?

He still wanted money though. Did she think he was some toy free with her packet of Frosties? It wasn't his fault if she chickened out, he'd taken a risk and she wouldn't want Malky to know now, would she? She put her dressing gown on and went to get her purse off the kitchen table. He wiped his hand down his jeans before he took it, as though he'd just touched something dirty. And the tosser wanted paid for doing the bathroom and all; he'd been reminding her of this when Hugh rung the doorbell.


Alison took another cigarette from the packet and tapped it against the box. She'd hoped she would've got through the last twenty minutes of this visit without coming back to the subject of Gordon, but no such luck.

Aye, I've seen him, she says. Once or twice.

I know, Malky says.

If you know, why'd you ask? Who told you? No, let me guess. Hugh.

She flicks open her lighter.

At least someone hasn't forgotten the meaning of loyalty, Malky says.

Oh, is that what you call it?

Not like Gordon. I used to think Gordon would take over the business from me.

Gordon's always been your favorite, hasn't he? Greedy

wee bugger, though.

Greedy? Well, well.

Malky's tone makes Allison decide to back-pedal a bit from slagging Gordon off.

But, he's no a bad boy, really, she says. Tries his best.

He's not a boy. Was old enough to know what he was doing.

What d'you mean?

You should've waited.

I *am* waiting.

We said we'd wait.

Allison's hand begins to shake. She stubs out her cigarette, and looks around the hall. She knows she'll remember this moment, squirrel it away into her memory box along with those other times in her life that came with a before and an after built in. She smells antiseptic, aftershave, and wet nylon, and something meaty from the prison canteen and even a whiff of Carol-Anne off the borrowed coat, and a tang of herself, of her own bleeding.

Malky leans forward. So, he whispers, you still afraid of heights?

She swallows, trembling.

He leans back and folds his arms.

We didn't know back then that you were going to get caught, but, she said. I was worried it'd be too late. By the time you get out, I'll be forty-two. Apart from yourself, Malky, it's the only thing I've ever wanted.

Tonight Allison will dream about Gordon. She'll dream about the doorbell ringing while he's in the middle of a critical ratcheting of the tap, about how he curses and puts his spanner down, the water drooling round the fixture's edge into the bath. He stands up, stiff from kneeling in his dusty jeans on Allison's fluffiest mat which she warned him time and again not to use, and pads out the bathroom, leaving tools scattered behind him, where they will lie for several hours before being gathered up and hand-me-downed. He embosses damp footprints on the hall runner to the front door and back, after letting his unexpected visitor in. He's no bothered by him, though, because it's someone he knows.

The rain slamming against the copper Victorian roof of Barlinnie churns up a racket inside the cavernous hall like the pistons of an enormous engine. Allison can barely hear herself think let alone talk. This must be what it was like to be one of those poor welders she remembers being told about at school, who got trapped and died inside the bellies of the big ocean liners they used to build on the Clyde.

She senses her make-up has smeared. Black tracks thread the tissues balled in her fist. She didn't wail back then on her birthday, but she's wailing now, bawling with the effort to be heard. Bubbling into her hanky like that poor woman from earlier.

And then the man from the council said they'd nudge me up the housing queue, she says, get me out the high rise if I was pregnant. Out to a proper house. They're starting to demolish some of the high rises now, but it'll be yonks afore they get round to mine.

She read in the paper how the council plans to move the locals out the more decrepit flats and use the space as temporary accommodation for the immigrants. Scotland's taking in victims of ethnic cleansing from the European Union and Africa. Ethnic cleansing always makes Allison imagine women and weans being chased by neds with Brillo pads. Her place is hoatching with Serbs and Somalis now, a sad-eyed bunch from countries where folk have turned revenge into an art form. They've brought their grievances with them into the high rises, but she won't tell Malky that, that she's frightened to go out at night in case she gets caught between them trying to finish over here what they'd started over there.

Malky's arms are still folded, his jittering right leg makes the table shudder.

And I know it's awful, but it seemed the perfect solution, she says. And Carol-Anne. Seeing her everywhere with that wean. It's no fair. Oh, Malky, I'm sorry, but it was a stupid idea, you know? You know how you can get an idea in the middle of the night and it makes perfect sense, common sense even.

She blows her nose and takes a deep breath.

It doesn't matter, but. Cause I changed my mind.

In Allison's dream, someone has moved her sofa from blocking the entrance to the veranda. No one has been out on the veranda since her granny died, but now the door swings open, the wind yo-yo-ing it back and forth slowly on its rusty hinges, and making the doorknob rub a chip in Jimmy's nicely hung new wallpaper.

The concrete floor of the balcony is sodden, the darkness beyond it punctured with lights. It showers in fits and starts, the wind tossing rain in handfuls into the living-room, where it smatters against the furniture like soggy confetti.

What d'ye mean, you changed your mind? Malky's leg stops jittering.

The best laid plans o' mice and men. She shrugs, and tries to smile.

But I thought you were...

I couldn't do it. It felt wrong. It was wrong.

Malky unfolds his arms and runs his palms down the sharp blade of his trouser crease. Allison picks up her bag.

So, that's that. Glad I got it off my chest, she says. Guess it's just going to be you and me, heh?

She takes a mirror compact from her bag and opens it to inspect the damage.

Oh, Jesus, look at my face. I'm like a Halloween cake.

She wipes her eyes, and tucks her hair behind her ears. A reflection appears of the guard behind her, and she snaps the compact shut.

Malky springs to his feet. What time is it? he says.

Where are you going?

I've got to make a call. He heads toward the prisoners' wing.

It's no four o'clock yet! Allison shouts after him. We've got ten minutes left!

The guard stops Malky at the door toward the prisoners' wings and points back to the chair.

I need to get to a phone, Malky says.

You've had your call, this week, son, sit yourself back down. Your tart's got herself all dolled up to come and see you.

That's right, Malky, says the other guard behind Allison. Show your bird some respect.

Malky walks slowly back and sits down.

Aye, says the first guard. And maybe the pair of you can gie us another song.

The Guards snigger and return to their positions. Allison leans across the table and rests her hand on Malky's arm.

What is it, love? Do you need me to tell someone something?

Doesn't matter.

Oh, come on, Malky don't be like that. God, I know I can be daft cow sometimes but I love you. Always have. Thick and thin. Sickness and health. Till death, and whatever. I mean it.

I know, hen. I know.

Sing us a song, then. They bampots asked for one, serves them right if they get it.

Malky shakes his head. Allison rakes through her memory, trying to think of one of their favorites that might cheer him up. I know, she says. Then starts singing.

*Won't you come see about me?*
*I'll be alone dancing, you know it will be me,*
*Tell me your troubles and doubts.*
*Giving me everything, inside and out.*
*Don't you forget about me, don't, don't, don't, don't you*

*forget about me.*
*Will you stand above me, look my way, never love me,*
*Rain keeps falling, rain keeps falling,*
*down, down, down …*
She stops when he doesn't join in.


Allison goes up the back of the bus to get a heat from the engine. The faces of most of the other passengers are familiar to her, she sees the same ones every month, but they just exchange a nod and look out the window. Everyone likes to be left in peace with their own thoughts after a visit to the Bar-L.

A nice hot bath when she gets home should deal with the remnants of the cramps, she thinks, Gordon should have installed the new taps by now. Malky took it really well, though, better than she thought. She snuggles down into the corner, cozily satisfied with the thumping depth of his love.

For once she's glad they never got married, because Malky's criminal record would have snookered their chances of adopting. As a single woman under forty, though, she can apply on her own. Some of her pals think adoption is like getting a wean second-hand, but that's nonsense. You've as much chance of being lumbered with a tear-away having your own kids as somebody else's. Those immigrants swarm with kids, maybe she'll end up with one of them. She couldn't care less what color it is. She'll print off the forms tomorrow in the computer lab at the school. She leans her head against the window and smiles. The red and yellow lights from the city smear across the glass. The pavements are black and slick like bin-liners.

She'll not be a brilliant ma, but she'd do her best, not only with the obvious stuff that everybody knows about, like making sure he or she doesn't eat too many sweeties, watch too much telly, and is read to every night, but with the other stuff she's learned from working with the kids at school. How kids need their own space, and not to be treated like half-wits, that it's important to be their mother, not their best pal.

The number 23 stops at the corner of Pollokshaws Road at the foot of the flats. Allison gets off. The rain has ended, so she folds her brolly and sticks it under her arm. The lights from an ambulance and a police car whirl at the entrance to the high rise, and two policemen are keeping a huddle of people back from a blanket thrown over something on the ground. Jesus Christ, she thinks, surely no another poor soul has jumped. The suicide rate has been atrocious of late, what with the drugs, and the drink, and the foreigners miserable with not being able to speak the language or wipe their memories of the things they've seen.

She recognizes the supermarket trolley parked at the side of the group, and Sorry's back hunched over it. His boyfriend's got his arm around him. Sorry's boyfriend is built like a tank and works as a bouncer at the clubs, which is why nobody dares take the mickey out the pair of them. The boyfriend's earrings glint in the dark, as he rubs Sorry's shoulders.

They turn at the sound of Allison's heels clacking against the pavement. Sorry straightens up and walks to meet her, leaving his boyfriend to stop the shopping cart from trundling backwards down the bray. Sorry's saying something, but she can't make it out because the wind fills her ears. It looks like an apology.

# Day of the Dead

TWO SERVANTS STRETCH the white canvas sail taut between the tamarind trees and secure it with sisal knots. Old Pedro turns on the first reel.

*SEE THE BARBARIC AUCTION OF BEAUTIFUL GIRLS*
*TO THE LORD OF ALGERIAN HAREMS!*
*SEE THE HEROINE, DISGUISED, INVADE*
*THE BEDOUINS SECRET SLAVE RITES!*

Esperanza turns to her great-grandmother for translation of these English titles, but Doña Maria Silva de Montillo selects a cigarillo from the enamelled box by her side and says nothing. Their wicker chairs are positioned on the veranda to enjoy the flickering images from the movie projector propped up on the cocktail cabinet behind them, its height augmented by the thick accounting book of the year's henequen plant production, the date "1921" etched in gold along its spine. One chair sits empty. Esperanza's mother, Josefa, is still in Roberto's bedroom, where Esperanza's younger brother lies ill.

The garden wall is striped oxblood and ochre stone. Beyond it, the plantation workers make their pilgrimage to the cemetery. They murmur to one another, carrying candles, limes and jacaranda blossoms. The sky is dark and clear. The outline of the hacienda's chimney reaches up through the palms to cup a waning moon, the white-washed initials "L.S.M." barely visible. Esperanza watches the procession snake around their periphery, fidgeting to follow and too wise to ask. Her great-grandmother tolerates the servants celebrating Día de Los Muertos, but considers it beneath the dignity of her family to take part in such a religiously suspect, and sensual, ritual.

Doña María's servant, Old Pedro, limps over to light her cigarillo. She has applied more powder to her face since dinner. It rises from her chalky profile and sits tremulous on her moustache, clouding the shoulders of the black crêpe gown first worn on the death of her mother in 1870, over fifty years before.

The two servants wait by the trees, having completed the complex ritual of knots. They wring their straw hats like washing, impatient to be gone. Doña María lifts a Dresden cup of cacao and chilli before dismissing them with a bony gesture. They streak into the darkness to join the ceremonies of Día de Los Muertos, the jungle swallowing the white flashes of their clothing. Meanwhile, Old Pedro lowers himself, accompanied as always by his martyrdom, to sit at his mistress's boney ankles.

Esperanza inches her chair beyond Doña María's peripheral vision, kicks off her shoes, and places her feet on the cool tile floor. Today, a few weeks after her twelfth birthday, she is no longer a child. The wads of cotton wrapped under her knickers feel moist and heavy, and she fears that her dress will stain. Pain claws up and down her abdomen.

"Grown, at last," her mother had said that morning. There was relief in her voice and she had squeezed Esperanza as though testing a mango for market. Esperanza's secret ripples through the hacienda. The nudgings of servants trail in her wake. She feels soiled and ashamed, resentful that her body can alter without her approval. Everyone finds her predicament funny. They save their sympathy for Roberto.

"Savages," Doña Maria says, shaking her head. Her cigarillo quivers at the end of a mottled hand. On the movie screen, sepia-toned men, in a fuss of cummerbunds and daggers, frown at a huddle of camels and tents.

Esperanza says nothing, having learned long ago not to question her great-grandmother's declamations against the vice in which she is, at that moment, thoroughly engrossed. She has been told that Doña Maria, at one hundred years of age, possesses wisdom beyond the normal ken. But the true north of Doña Maria's moral compass often appears off kilter to Esperanza; her pronouncements on manners, religion, and society spin and judder from day to day.

It is unusual to be at the hacienda in November. Normally, the family returns to Mérida during the rainy season to allow Esperanza and Roberto to resume their studies. Their father, Doña Maria's grandson, Luis Silva, had not visited the hacienda on Esperanza's birthday, but had come in September for Roberto's seventh. During the excitement of the hot air balloon ride, Luis Silva skirted all enquiries regarding this change from the familiar routine.

"I will write," he had said, cantering away into an afternoon storm.

The children's tutor, Señor Mendoza, arrived unannounced from Mérida at the beginning of October. Esperanza's mother rushed to furnish a storage room, as the hacienda was not designed for hospitality. Lessons are now held on the buttermilk-colored veranda that fulfils the function of dining room and drawing room and runs the extensive length between the foreman's office and the chapel. Open completely on one side to the lawn, its checkerboard tiles and ceiling fans help to mitigate the stalking aggression of the heat. Awnings are lowered on rainy days to shield the equestrian paintings and fine furniture from harm.

Señor Mendoza only appears for lessons and dinner.

He spends the remainder of his time hiding from Esperanza's mother's rising misery and the hovering indignation of Doña Maria that is always looking for a soft place to land. Every morning, Esperanza and Roberto watch the tutor's mincing progress from his room to the veranda, his fleshy torso tipped forward as though his shoes perpetually pinch. His whiskered face hides behind a handkerchief clutched against the stench of the henequen and sweat stains flower under the armpits of his too-fitted suits. Esperanza and Roberto breathe easily in the putrid air and wait for him to catch his breath. During the lesson, his words scamper forth pell-mell between gulps into the safety of the cloth.

Esperanza glances at the door to Señor Mendoza's room. It is firmly shut. Roberto's bedroom is similarly sealed. She sighs and shifts her weight, the chair creaking under her, and props her elbow on the arm to balance her chin on her palm. Her gaze drifts back to the screen as a smoky-eyed man enters the frame and the camera lingers to allow the audience to catch and hold their breath. Her great-grandmother greets his appearance with something between a snort and a sigh. Esperanza finds his features attractive but reserved. She can't tell what he is thinking. He looks like her father; Luis Silva's face, too, is handsome and blank. It is unlikely that the family will return to Mérida now, she thinks, glancing back to Roberto's door. Not now that her father's mistress is living in the family mansion on the elegant Calle de Montejo.

It was two weeks before that the discovery had been made. Esperanza's mother, Josefa, had declared that she could wait no longer for Luis Silva to instruct the family to return to Mérida. The damp and heat were proving unbearable.

The latest caravan of henequen was ready to journey through the jungle to the sea and the protection of an entourage appealed to Josefa. Despite the new government, Mexico was still lawless and dissolute following years of revolution. The rope-wrapped trunks that had cluttered the rooms for many weeks were finally loaded onto the carriage.

Striding back and forth, her low-waisted dress emphasizing a boyish figure, Josefa directed Esperanza and Roberto to collect last minute trinkets before pulling a straw cloche over her wiry hair. Doña Maria stood on the veranda watching the servants bustle ineffectively around. She leaned both hands on her cane and looked down at her grandson's small, Mayan wife.

"I refuse to come with you," she said, even though she hadn't been asked.

Their mother ushered Esperanza and Roberto into the carriage, impatient as always to be somewhere else. As the carriage pulled away to join the caravan, Doña Maria shouted behind them.

"And I don't know why you don't use the automobile!"

The automobile was Doña Maria's current favorite grievance. She greeted every new invention with revulsion before insisting that its convenience be immediately and ruthlessly exploited. The motion picture, the typewriter, the icebox, and now the automobile had run her gauntlet from ridicule to necessity. But the road to Mérida was still unpaved, and the automobile that had, at her insistence, been dragged by mules from the port at Progresso, festered in a stable. Luis Silva's fear for its delicate axles condemned its chrome and livery to the greedy mold of the Yucatán, and the cream leather seats had long since welcomed armadillos and rattlers.

The journey to Mérida took four hours. To Esperanza, it was interminable. Long, straight and muddy, the dirt track was peppered with pools of water from October's relentless rains. Shrubby rows of henequen plants stretched to the flat horizon interspersed with the rubble of ancient structures that Roberto, boisterous and ruddy-faced, squirmed to climb.

They traveled first through her mother's village of

Chunchucmil—deserted, as most of the men were working in the fields. Josefa stared straight ahead, toes tapping and twirling her parasol in lively hands. Then through Granada, Chochola and Uman, all sharing a similar straggle of thatched huts, with doorless entranceways and glassless windows, holding hammocks and little else. A mother lay breast-feeding in one; an old man dozed in another. They crossed the ditch where Esperanza had seen the decaying corpse of a soldier the year before. She remembered the veil of flies that had lifted as they passed.

Esperanza distracted Roberto by pointing out wild turkeys and playing word games to keep him from clambering around and ruining her dress. She wanted to look pretty for her father. Ahead and behind them, the henequen swayed in great bails, ripe for transformation into carpets or rope and tenacious enough to rig ships and lynchings. On its receipt in New Orleans, Señor Cortez, her father's agent, would send back the latest motion picture in a metal casket accompanied by a letter hinting at its decadent delights. Her mother once told Esperanza that Señor Cortez was an old beau of Doña Maria. Although he must be at least thirty years younger, she had added with a laugh. Doña Maria kept the letters from Señor Cortez in an old humidor. One afternoon Esperanza had peaked inside. The letters, boring and demure, were saturated by the scent of pomade.

The convoy of henequen left them at Mérida and they continued unescorted past the bulky cathedral and around Hidalgo Square, before entering the oak-lined Calle de Montejo. The carriage's weary appearance and burden of trunks drew stares.

The family home was the color of a blue sky dipped in milk. It stood further back from the avenue than its neighbors, behind an ornate iron balustrade and wrapped in palm and bougainvillea. Its roof and windows were decorated with carved wood painted white. The gates opened after some delay, revealing Emilio, Luis Silva's manservant, standing at the top of the marble stairway that poured down to lap at the lawn. His face was creased with unhappiness.

Her mother started to leave the carriage before it had shuddered to a halt. Then, Esperanza saw her father. Luis Silva paused for a moment at the door with his hand on Emilio's shoulder. The two men exchanged remarks before Emilio disappeared into the house. With one hand behind his back, Esperanza's father walked slowly down the stairs. He moved, as always, as though to invite her mother to dance.

Luis Silva was the most beautiful man Esperanza had ever seen. The midday sun gilded his pale skin, lifted his dark hair from the shadows and threaded it through with copper. Taller than the other men on the hacienda, matched only by his business acquaintances who choked the dining room with cigars, he paused a step or two above her mother, his upright bearing elongating the slender waist and hips.

Esperanza had once heard their cook, Magdalena, describe Luis Silva as blond. She hadn't understood the word but assumed it encompassed not only that strange void between herself and her father, but his ability to draw and hold all eyes in a room while saying and doing nothing. On those few occasions when his gaze met hers, or he lightly touched her hair, her body would tense and ache. Afterwards, it would mourn. Perhaps this glistening, she thought, this ability to cause others to yearn to die a little, is blond. Later she realized that Magdalena meant, simply, that Luis Silva was Spanish.

He was less elegantly dressed than usual. He wore no overcoat. His white shirt was unbuttoned at neck and cuffs and carelessly tucked into riding breeches. Esperanza's mother stretched to embrace him. Catching both her hands in his, he kissed one and then the other before laying them gently by her side. Esperanza pulled Roberto in front of her to get out of the carriage.

"Stay where you are," Luis Silva called. She hesitated

and sat down again, jerking Roberto back by the coat tails. "I didn't send for you," he said to her mother, "and I can't believe you brought them with you."

Light blinked behind him in the cool darkness. A slender shape slipped past the arched windows at the end of the entrance hall.

"She's here, isn't she?" Josefa's hand rose to her mouth. Her parasol dropped down the steps in a slow clatter.

"Take them back," Luis Silva said.

Josefa stared beyond him into the gloom. "She is living here."

Esperanza grasped her mother's meaning in an instant but resisted its implications, grinding her heels into the wooden boards on the carriage floor. Her girlfriends in Mérida whispered about such things, whipping themselves into intoxicated giggles when huddled in the corner of the library or behind white-gloved hands in the park. She felt nauseous with shame.

Roberto's confusion turned to panic. Esperanza gripped him strongly, causing him to squirm and complain. Her father came down to the carriage. Esperanza didn't want to look at him but couldn't turn away. He took Roberto's head in his hands and their blue eyes met in communion.

"Remember, you are hacendado till I come home," he said, kissing Roberto on both cheeks. Roberto's face crumpled and his panic peaked in tears. Esperanza pulled him into the crook of her arm and covered his pale fingers with her own darker hand. She whispered to him to be quiet as he choked, dragged his nose along the sleeve of her best dress. Luis Silva turned to help Josefa back into the carriage, but she jerked her arm out of his grasp. He stepped away with a slight bow and tucked both his hands behind him.

Only Esperanza had glanced back as the carriage left the shade of the garden for the Calle de Montejo. Her father was gone. He had said nothing to her. The front door was closed. Her mother's parasol lay on the marble steps.

And so the carriage had retraced its route. They passed the mansion with a carving of a conquistador standing on the heads of two Indians. Roberto failed to point at it and giggle as he was apt to do, and even the bustling marketplace couldn't raise him from his torpor.

The road back to the hacienda stretched before them through a tunnel of heat. Steam rose from the drying soil; mosquitoes swirled under their hats. One servant drove the carriage while the other sat on the rear footplate, watching their receding tracks. Both men had rifles slung over their shoulders. They chewed tobacco and spat sullenly into the ditches. Roberto fell asleep, puffy lids closed over his father's eyes and he nodded rhythmically against Esperanza's shoulder. She studied the unchanging view, furious at her father's behaviour yet eager to forgive, and embarrassed by her mother's tears pouring unchecked in front of the servants, in front of her own children.

When they returned through Chunchucmil, a woman paused at the side of the road to let them pass. She carried a pail of water and balanced a baby boy against her hip. Josefa pleaded for the driver to stop. The carriage stuttered and halted.

The two women stared at one another. The driver muttered something to the servant on the footplate causing both men to laugh. He returned his gaze to the horses' flanks and fanned himself, lazily, with his hat.

Esperanza's mother talked to the woman in Mayan. The woman put the pail down and lifted the child up to the carriage and into Josefa's arms. Josefa ran her fingers through the boy's thick hair and round the brows of his unblinking blue eyes. As her mother gave him back, his chubby hand grabbed at the rose silk shawl around her neck and would not let it go. Josefa ignored the woman's rising protestations. She is telling her to keep it, Esperanza thought, forgetting to feel annoyed in her surprise. Esperanza had often admired this particular shawl and had hoped her mother would allow her to wear it.

The woman pried the boy's fingers away from the silk. Ignoring his howl of protest, she looped the shawl around her neck and swept one end over her shoulder before picking up the pail and walking away. They disappeared into a hut with a goat tethered by the door.

Josefa tapped the driver's back. "Go on," she said.

The carriage lurched forward. Josefa removed her filigree and coral earrings and turned them over in her palm, her body swaying with the gait. "Something else I could easily live without."

Esperanza looked at the earrings. She felt trapped by Josefa's anger. Anything she said would be perceived as impertinence, yet to say nothing would frustrate her mother more.

"She was pretty," her mother said. "Wasn't she?"

Esperanza nodded. The woman had been small and dark like her mother, but with a younger, more tired expression.

"She's my sister."

Esperanza had never seen her mother's sister. Indeed, her mother's family were rarely mentioned. She twisted around to catch another glimpse of this new found aunt, but the village had been swallowed into the bush. The view behind was identical to the one ahead.

"That's enough." Josefa slapped her roundly on the arm.

Esperanza turned back to the relentlessly bland landscape, leaving a small trickle of blood to run down her wrist where her mother's nail had nicked a trail. The remainder of the journey passed in silence. Her mother shed no more tears, but lifted her chin in a familiar gesture indicating that some decision had been made.

When the carriage finally came to rest at the hacienda, Doña Maria appeared in the doorway of the chapel holding a black lace fan. A servant helped Esperanza and Josefa climb out, their dresses encrusted with sweat and dust. Roberto attempted to stand but dropped drowsily down again. He leaned over the side of the carriage and retched.

"So," Doña Maria said, her fan smacking the air. "You came back."

Esperanza is disappointed in this heroine. She finds her too pale and too fat. The actress has bow lips and strides up and down in riding breeches. Her eyebrows are exaggerated. Her mouth is open. Nothing is heard.

*MARRIAGE IS THE END OF INDEPENDENCE,*
*I AM CONTENT WITH MY LIFE AS IT IS.*

Doña Maria hesitates a moment before translating this blasphemous line into Spanish. Esperanza suspects that her great-grandmother finds the riding breeches impertinent too, but there they are. She lifts herself, gingerly, and goes in search of her mother. Doña Maria will be vexed at being abandoned, but is too titillated by the escalating drama to follow her.

Esperanza walks through the archway from the veranda into the kitchen over cobbles pillaged from the surrounding ruins. Magdalena, the cook, stands on a small stool, clearing away the debris from the preparation of the Dish of Spirits. She sweeps scraps of ground meat, flour, cocoa beans, and maize husks off the large oak table into a bucket. A small dish of tamale, decorated with cilantro, sits at one end next to a jug of tanchucuá. Magdalena will take these with her later to place on the graves of her ancestors, the rest having gone ahead with the other servants to the cemetery. Magdalena smiles toothlessly and lifts her petticoat to step down off the stool. She pours a glass of tanchucuá and gives it to Esperanza, reaching up to pat her cheek with a wrinkled hand.

Esperanza sips, inhaling aniseed and honey. Laughter and singing hover beyond the open garden door. She hears her mother's brisk footsteps on the cobbles as she enters the kitchen, carrying a bowl smeared with a rancid green paste.

"Can't I go?" Esperanza asks. They argue every year over Día de Los Muertos.

"You should be keeping Doña Maria company," Josefa says.

Esperanza knows it's easier to live by Doña Maria's rules than thwart them. She shrugs and turns an enquiring gaze toward Magdalena who shakes her head. In the past, Magdalena helped Esperanza sneak out to the cemetery for she believes Esperanza has the gift of communing with the dead. Esperanza is sceptical but enjoys the fuss.

Magdalena will not help her this evening because Roberto is ill. Not only is he her father's favourite, he has managed to spoil one of the best nights of the year—she should feel bad about having such thoughts, but she can't help it. Her mother says something in Mayan to Magdalena, then dumps the bowl into the sink. Magdalena nods and turns to the stove to stir a pot of boiling water, adding pink petals all the while.

"Can I see him?" Esperanza hasn't seen Roberto for two days.

"Later." Her mother stretches to get a clean dish off the dresser.

"Is he very sick?"

Her mother places the dish on the table, before wrapping one arm around Esperanza's waist, and kissing her lightly on the forehead. Taking the glass of tanchucuá from Esperanza's hand, she lifts it to her lips and gulps it back. Bruised hollows cup her eyes and sweat bleeds between her breasts. Esperanza enjoys this rare intimacy but senses that she does not have her mother's full attention. Her fingers trace the worn knots of the kitchen table.

"Shouldn't we send for a doctor?" she asks. Her mother's arm drops from her waist.

"Go sit with Doña Maria. You know how she hates to spend her evenings without an audience."

Over the years, Esperanza had peeked through the banisters of their Mérida home to spy on parties strangely bereft of guests. She had sat at breakfast, her head aching from one hundred strokes of the brush, and listened to her mother read the polite refusals for society or charity events she had planned. Her father would stir his coffee, flick open his newspaper and say nothing. Some of the servants lavished her mother with an affection that Doña Maria found unseemly while others failed to doff their hats when she passed by. Esperanza had come to understand that her parents' marriage had not been a success, as viewed from every rung of society's ladder. Her father was a Spanish gentleman who had married a Mayan peasant. To some, this was odd, to others, inexcusable.

On days when Señor Mendoza forgot to wake up after his siesta, Esperanza and Roberto would sneak out of the hacienda and into the small village that hugged its walls to visit their grandfather. The children had come to know him through his gifts, deposited at the foreman's office every birthday and Christmas, although the hand-hewn toys wrapped in newspaper were rarely given more than a passing glance.

Esperanza knew that her mother was aware of these illicit visits but chose to say nothing. Her grandfather had not seen his daughter since Josefa's marriage to the hacendado over thirteen years before, and although he sometimes asked the children about her, he never asked more than one question at a time. He did not need to; Esperanza always responded to his single queries with many, many answers. She refused to accept that a father could be so indifferent to his daughter's life.

Her grandfather lived at the end of the village before the dirt track skirted the skeleton of the old hacienda Santa Helena. It had been razed to the ground during Pancho Villa's last rampage through the Yucatán, and only its chimney stood intact. In its shadow, her grandfather's hut badly needed to be re-thatched. The palm fronds unravelled over its rim like a fraying serape.

Indoors, a small torn picture of the Virgin Mary hung on the wall next to the hammock. Tacked alongside was a fading photograph of the peasant rebel leader, Emeliano Zapata, cut tidily from a newspaper. Short and ugly, Zapata stands, leans almost, against an exhausted-looking nag buckling under a millstone of weapons and sacks. He looks directly at the camera with panicked yet defiant eyes.

It was just such souvenirs of the revolution that drove Roberto to goad Esperanza to take him to see their grandfather. She wanted to go anyway, but preferred to pretend to be persuaded. The village was slovenly, rank with vegetable peelings and open sewers, and the local children, frank and hostile, shadowed their movements.

A couple of days before their fruitless journey to Mérida, Esperanza had swung in her grandfather's hammock, her shoes off and her sailor dress bunched above her knees, her sturdy brown legs stretched akimbo. She watched her grandfather and Roberto through the doorless entranceway, sword fighting with blunt machetes in the dust. Chickens pecked indifferently around their feet.

Esperanza's grandfather raised his arms in surrender. He had a thin body, wiry from working so many years in the fields, and three fingers missing on his left hand due to an accident while hacking at the broad, muscular stocks of the henequen. His neck rattled about in the stiff shell of his starched white shirt, the rolled-up sleeves revealing arms as slim and sinuous as her mother's. But where Josefa's were smooth as brown eggs, her grandfather's were the texture of turtle hide.

"And that is how Zapata would fight," he said in broken Spanish.

"Why did he die?" Roberto knew the answer. His grandfather had recounted the story of Zapata's assassination many times before.

"We all die." Grandfather sat down on the threshold

and rubbed one hand through his thick white hair.

"But, why?" Roberto asked again, using the machete to trace his name in the dirt. His hands were rust-stained and he kept wiping them down his trousers. Esperanza had sneaked him into the kitchen and cleaned him up when they'd returned home. Her mother would have been livid at the state of his appearance, her anger fuelled by fear of the strange maladies that continued to ferment in the countryside in the wake of the revolution and famine. Occasionally they rose to the surface like bile.

"Weren't they on the same side?" Roberto persisted.

Grandfather signalled Roberto to come and sit beside him. He took the machete from Roberto's hands and tossed it away. "Side—causes—such things no longer matter," he said. "When the fighting begins—revenge is everything."

Esperanza senses that Doña Maria finds this latest motion picture deliciously scandalous. Her great-grandmother lights another cigarillo with shaky hands and sweeps ash off her bodice. Señor Cortez had sent a decorous note along with the reels. It lies open on top of the metal canister. *My most cherished Doña Maria Silva de Montillo*, the letter says, his writing, as always, according to her mother, slaked with tequila. *I have snatched this latest entertainment for you, as soon as ever I could. But I must warn you, my most revered Señora, aware as I am of your delicate sensibilities, that "The Sheik" has caused not a little scandal here.*

Esperanza's mother appears at Roberto's bedroom door. She pauses a moment, then closes it softly behind her. She walks across the lawn carrying a pitcher and a pile of linen, taking care not to obstruct the beam from the projector before disappearing down the passageway to the kitchen. Esperanza places both hands over her stomach. She feels sick. Soon, she hears her mother return and straighten the orchestra of silverware adorning the buffet on the veranda. The candles gutter as Josefa begins a rhythmical pacing behind Esperanza and Doña Maria. Eventually she stops and taps Esperanza on the shoulder.

"Sit up straight," she says.

### WHY HAVE YOU BROUGHT ME HERE?

The smoky-eyed man in biblical dress, with no lips and a chiselled profile, kneads the podgy heroine about the torso. A large insect lands on the screen and crawls across the heroine's vacant face.

### ARE YOU NOT WOMAN ENOUGH TO KNOW?

"Suitable entertainment for a young girl, Doña Maria," says Josefa.

Esperanza is surprised by this remark. Her mother rarely bothers about Doña Maria's moving-picture shows. Besides, no one cares when Esperanza watches the grooms corralling her father's stud with the mares for breeding.

"I think I can be the judge of what is, or is not, suitable entertainment," Doña Maria replies without turning her head. Nevertheless, she refrains from translating the next two titles into Spanish.

"Perhaps you could share your wisdom with your grandson." Josefa paces back and forth.

"He seems quite determined to make his own mistakes. It is not my place to interfere. Not yours either."

"Didn't your husband, the great Don Silva de Montillo, have a mistress?"

Doña Maria's head turns to one side. Her hawkish profile sits black against the screen. Her nostrils and mouth twitch. Esperanza is suddenly aware of all the sounds from the surrounding bush, the hissing, chattering and mocking of a million living things.

"Did she live in your home?" Josefa whispers into the heavy air. "And sleep in your bed?" She turns on her heels and walks briskly back to Roberto's room. The door closes behind her.

Doña Maria hands claw over the arms of her chair. A dog howls from the village and then quietens with a sob. Old Pedro dozes at Doña Maria's feet, his head bobbing as he hugs his chest. Doña Maria picks up her cane and cracks him on the shoulder.

"Wake up!" she says, "Change the reel."

A letter had arrived from Mérida this morning, while Esperanza and her mother sat at breakfast on the veranda, the only meal of the day taken without Doña Maria's company. She always ate breakfast in her room, floundering among pillows in the enormous mahogany bed, surrounded by Goya miniatures and dried bouquets under glass from her glory days in Madrid.

On the lawn in front of the foreman's office, the hacienda workers waited silently in wavy queues, to receive payment vouchers for the previous week's labor. They rarely glanced at Esperanza or her mother on the veranda in front of them. Their wives also waited, leaning against the garden wall or squatting under the palms, ready to take the vouchers to the factory store and exchange them for sacks of rice and beans.

A linen napkin lay on Josefa's lap. She lifted a knife to slice open the envelope, her eyes ashy from another night by Roberto's bedside, her wiry hair clipped loosely at her neck. Esperanza concentrated on lifting the silver coffeepot, her wrist shaking with the weight as she poured coffee into her mother's cup. Jars of French preserves, a bowl of papayas and a vase of fiery orchids sat on the table.

"I've been such a fool." Her mother dropped the letter onto her plate.

Doña Maria's bedroom door opened, and she stepped frowning into the sunlight. She carried a book and a rosary. The workers whipped off their hats.

"You're not drinking coffee, I hope, Esperanza?" she

said as she paused by the table. "It's a filthy, heathen concoction" She lifted the lid off the pot to see if there was any left. Esperanza glanced at her mother. "Josefa, your hair is particularly unbecoming this morning." Doña Maria picked a morsel from Esperanza's plate but paused before putting it in her mouth. "What's the matter—what's happened to the boy?"

"Nothing has happened to the boy." Josefa raised her head. Doña Maria noticed the letter. Josefa covered it with her hand. "Luis is not coming home," she said.

"That's certainly not a reason to appear slatternly at breakfast." Doña Maria wiped her fingers on a napkin and picked up her book again. "I hope this will be an end to your appalling conduct over the last few days," she continued, and then paused as a servant appeared. The servant lifted the empty plates from the table and returned to the kitchen. "May I remind you," her words slithered out between her teeth as her eyes scanned the lawn, "that you married into this family and therefore owe us a debt of loyalty?"

"Loyalty." Josefa yanked her chair away causing the china cups to rattle. Esperanza stretched out her arms to steady them. Josefa's napkin dropped on the floor as she brushed past Doña Maria and headed toward the hacendado's quarters. Her walk broke into a run.

Doña Maria contemplated picking up the letter, but decided against it under Esperanza's persistent stare. Instead she walked stiffly to the chapel where she spent part of every day, praying in front of the wooden statue of the Virgin Mary draped in blossoms and rosaries. One afternoon, in an air murky with incense, Esperanza had found Doña Maria slumped on the second pew, her face alert for slights even in repose. Her book lay by her feet. Esperanza had flicked through it, pausing to scan its more racy passages, before closing it in confusion and disgust. It made her feel excited yet dirty and its existence in her great grandmother's lap in the chapel was one more inexplicable paradox.

Esperanza remained alone at the breakfast table. The first signs of maturity gnawed at her womb and she was apprehensive of its meaning. She picked up the letter and swept over her father's usual list of domestic instructions, before pausing at its concluding paragraph.

*Regarding Roberto, I am very concerned. I am sending Dr. Rodriguez from Mérida to attend him and I want you to follow his instructions without question. Do not treat him with any of your own remedies or allow Magdalena near him. Dr. Rodriguez has newly arrived from Mexico City and is already well respected here. Indeed, I found that we both attended university in Sevilla.* Esperanza brushed her fingers over the courtly signature, folded the letter and tucked it into her pocket.

But when Dr. Rodriguez arrived late that afternoon, in a rattling old automobile whose canvas roof was yawning under the weight of a Yucatán downpour, Esperanza's mother sent him away without allowing him to see Roberto.

"He needs his father," she had told him.

The last movie reel whirrs. The smoky-eyed man draws near the heroine who quakes in the corner of a tent. He advances in the way that Esperanza has seen her father approach the altar at communion, carefully and with reverence. His cloak falls from his shoulders as he walks, revealing a slim figure in a collarless tunic. A dagger hangs at his waist. His eyes are dark, heavy-lidded and unblinking. The heroine cowers like an animal. Esperanza is disturbed yet mesmerized and tries to imagine what it would feel like to have that fathomless gaze fixed on her. She wonders if her mother has noticed his resemblance to her father and turns to see Josefa standing in the shadows, watching the screen. The man lifts the heroine into his arms in one swift, effortless gesture and lays her down gently on large embroidered cushions. She struggles without conviction.

"My grandson will be here this evening." Doña Maria's words float from her wicker chair. Josefa turns her back to the screen. "I sent for him this morning." Doña Maria stands up carefully and turns around leaning on her cane. She whips her skirts behind her. For a moment she obstructs the beam and the image of a seduction ripples across her body.

"Turn that abomination off," she says. Old Pedro rises with many sighs and flicks the switch on the projector. The garden plunges into darkness. Drumming is heard from the cemetery. Doña Maria crosses the lawn to meet Josefa. She stops when they are close enough to embrace.

"Do you think I don't know what you've been doing to that boy?" Doña Maria lifts her cane to point first at Josefa and then the kitchen. "You and that peasant." She is about to continue but notices that Esperanza still sits in her chair. Esperanza folds her arms and stays where she is.

Doña Maria tugs at Josefa's sleeve. Josefa pulls away, hesitates for a moment, but then follows the older woman deeper into the garden. Under the trees, the two women stop and begin to talk together and at once. Their conversation crashes in waves, each voice breaks over the other before it, in turn, is pulled back and drowned.

Esperanza's breathing rises and falls with the argument as she sits on the verge of the darkness. Old Pedro squats down on his haunches and rolls a tatty string of tobacco into a creased cigarette paper. He ignores the women in the way that Esperanza's grandfather ignores the chickens that squabble around his door. An occasional phrase reaches Esperanza, breaking through the racket of drumming and insects.

Her mother's voice rises in denial that she would ever do such a thing. Doña Maria doubts Josefa's words, scepticism visible in every twitch of her body. And now my little sister too, Josefa continues, will it never end? Doña

Maria tosses disdain in the direction of the village while Josefa draws her breath to disagree. Esperanza misses her mother's reply.

It is a mistake, Doña Maria responds. She is adamant now that it is just a mistake. Her jet earrings flick in certainty, as though she knows the world rests on some slight of hand. A mistake? Josefa snorts that it was not a mistake she'd made. Oh, no. She points at her breast and declares that she'd made sure he'd married her. She wasn't going to be just another hacendado whore.

Doña Maria stumbles toward the veranda. She throws words over her shoulder. What he could have been, she shouts. He was a fool. A fool. She stops and leans heavily on her cane. She places a hand over her heart and turns back to Josefa, who still stands under the trees. Esperanza senses her great-grandmother is collecting ammunition for her next assault, but her mother takes this opportunity to spring to the offensive and walks briskly to Doña Maria's side.

"Don't avenge your marriage with mine," she says. The cicadas fall silent. The words tremble like crystal then shatter over the lawn.

It looks as though Doña Maria may strike Josefa. Her bony hand rises from her heart and then falters, falls. She shakes with rage. Spittle trembles on her lips. Esperanza's mother covers her mouth and flinches, awaiting the blow.

"I hope that boy dies," Dona Maria hisses. Her head bends forward and down like a cock in a pit. "Then Luis will see you for what you are."

Señor Mendoza's door opens slightly and then closes again. The cicadas chatter resumes. Josefa staggers onto the veranda as though drunk and enters the passage to the kitchen. The quick retort of her footsteps snaps then fades.

Doña Maria gestures to Old Pedro. He snuffs his cigarette between two fingers behind his back and returns the stub to his pocket. He limps over to her side and offers her his shoulder to lean on, then guides her to her room. Esperanza remains in her rattan chair, her knees drawn up to her heart.

Roberto sweats profusely. Josefa moves him to the casa de máquinas, where the henequen plant is threshed and stripped down to twine. She asks Esperanza to help her. Followed by Magdalena, they carry him wrapped in a blanket across the lawn and through the towering mahogany doors of the factory.

Magdalena lights a gas lamp at one end and turns on the huge ceiling fans that splice the air like the oars of a galleon. Josefa removes Roberto's blanket then lays him naked on the cool stone floor. She folds the blanket under his head and sponges his body with water before lying down beside him, to whisper endearments to his lips, his hair and his frantic eyes that follow her own as though attached with invisible cords.

Magdalena sets up a makeshift altar at one end of the factory, and props up a crucifix between two candles. She begins to mumble in prayer. Esperanza kneels in the corner by the window, unable to stop shaking. Roberto's body is gaunt with days of vomiting and diarrhea while his stomach, neck and wrists are puffy and blotched. His spine forms a bridge over the floor and his arms and legs spasm at the whim of an invisible puppeteer.

After a while, her mother helps Roberto to urinate into a bowl that Esperanza holds. His urine is fuchsia from the broth of bougainvillaea and tea.

It is almost midnight. The celebration of Día de los Muertos approaches its climax in the cemetery. Esperanza stands at her bedroom window in the dark, watching the lights jostle beyond the garden wall. Her mother had instructed her to go to bed but she cannot sleep. The main gates slam and she runs to peek around the door.

Her father crosses the lawn and hands the reins of his

horse to Mario, who leads it, steaming, toward the stable. Luis Silva walks stiffly from so many hours in the saddle. His elegance is drained and his teeth worry his lower lip. Esperanza leaves her room and follows him to the casa de máquinas and pauses in the gloom as he shoulders the mahogany door ajar.

Roberto lies naked on the floor. His body is still. His eyes are open and stare at the corner, where Esperanza's mother crouches in the darkness of the guttering lamp. Her shadow bruises the whitewashed adobe wall. From the cemetery, the celebration flares with laughter and a sudden whirling of fiddles and guitars.

Esperanza's father kneels by Roberto and gently closes his eyes. He looks at his wife though it is obvious to Esperanza that her mother cannot see him. Josefa's revenge is so mighty it has astonished her.

Esperanza hugs the doorframe a moment longer before returning to the garden. She leaves her parents with their quarrel lying lifeless between them and heads toward the cemetery, to the music and noise of the living.

She does not understand them and does not wish to. Her brother lies dead. Surely that is enough.

# Hell Mend You

WHEN I WAS WEE we used to play a game called "Happy Families." The pack had forty-four cards, 11 sets of a Ma, a Da, a son and a daughter. We only used the ten sets, but, because our mutt, Teddy Bear, chewed up Mistress Bung, wife of Bung the Brewer, leaving one family mother-less, and therefore useless in the game. Whoever collected the most families won.

The cards belonged to Uncle Harry. He used to play the game with my Ma, then she taught it to us. The pack was ancient. Scabby round the edges, with smooth oily bruises in the middle from being handled too many times. A long-gone box so we held them the-gether using an elastic band. They had creepy drawings on the front of dwarfy-people with cruel faces and big heads wobbling above tiny bodies, all dressed like something from *Upstairs Downstairs* and holding stuff to do with the family business. I mind a few of the names; there was Dose, the Doctor, and Tape, the Tailor, and Chip, the Carpenter—his wife held a hammer, huge as a pick-axe—and Bones, the Butcher, whose Mrs. carried a hatchet and had a face like a Tory MP, and his lassie was chewing on a bone.

Sometimes we'd all play: me, my Ma, my Da, my sister Sheena, and my brother Billy. But mostly it was Ma and Billy, though, according to the rules you were supposed to have at least three players. I wasn't that fussed to be honest. Looking at they cards, I couldn't help thinking our family must be skee-whiff somehow, because there were five of us, not four—because we had one kid too many.

## The Hand Dealt

That nosy cow downstairs must have called the police. My clothes were still damp and bloody when they arrived. I slung one of my Da's old cardigans over my halter-top and trackies. My feet were ringing wet and all, so I borrowed my Ma's cork-soled sandals which was a bummer 'cause my polish was chipped. She was taken off to Emergency, I couldn't very well stop that from happening, but I threw a fit when they wouldn't let me keep our Archie. Some constable bundled him away, half-dragging him, half-carrying him, squalling and squirming in her arms. She looked like she'd never even seen a wean before, let alone one determined to swim his way to freedom. They took me to Parkhead Station and dumped me in an interview room.

I was left on my own-e-o for over an hour, numb-bumed on a jaggy plastic chair, and hungry, without so much as a Milky Way. The table was chipped Formica with a yellow pattern like scrambled eggs, and I'd nothing to read. Finally a stunted barrel of a lassie arrives wearing a black suit with a skirt no much bigger than a hankie. She must have been freezing; it was a cold night.

"Are you no freezing?" I said, when she came in. "You'll catch your death."

She didn't look much older than me, maybe early thirties. A tall lanky policeman in uniform was at her tail, with a face like a wet Monday. My first guess would have been Laurel and Hardy, but she introduced herself as an Inspector Docherty, and he was a Sergeant MacIntyre. The Sergeant closed the door of the interview room that carefully you'd have thought it was triggered to explode.

"There's no use turning that thing on, hen," I said, nodding at the tape recorder on the desk when she sat down. "I'll no break till Cracker gets here. "

"Do you find this funny, Miss Ferguson?"

"I find families funny, Inspector. I'm trying to inject a little levity into the proceedings," I said, in my best toffee voice. "Encourage you to appreciate the spectacle of the human comedy in action." I leaned forward. "Between you and me, hen, I think yous are making a lot of fuss o'er nothing. I take it yous've all got bugger all else to do. There's a war going on in Easterhouse all the time, by the way, if you're looking for glory. Folk win medals just for living round there. Apache-land, so it is."

The skinny-malinky Sergeant put his head down and smiled.

"Isn't that right, Sergent?"

The Inspector looked at him. He smartened himself up.

"Aren't you going to ask how your mother is?" She said.

"I know how my mother is, thank you."

"Her nose is broken."

"I'd gathered that." I opened up my Da's cardigan and held my arms wide to let her see the state of my Juicy halter. I looked like a Tarantino extra.

The Inspector stared at my top like it was a big ink spot test and she was determined to winkle something out the splatters—Elvis, a willy, the meaning of life, who knows. We sat there saying nothing for so long I could feel my hair grow. This must be the silent treatment, I thought, I'm supposed to no be able to shut up.

"How's Archie?" I said. "He's a wee toe-rag, so he is. Probably been babbling a lot of nonsense."

The Inspector put her elbows on the table and rested her chin on her hands. The Sergeant, watery-eyed and dangle-jawed, was staring down at his tie, like his dog had just died.

"Where's your father, Miss Ferguson?"

"Haven't a Scooby. But I doubt he's thirsty. He'll be having one too many. It's no the first time and it'll no be the last."

"You think he had something to do with this, is that what you're saying?"

"He wasn't there."

"He was seen leaving your parents' flat before we arrived."

"You know," I said to the Inspector, while pointing at the Sergeant. "He'd have made a fortune in the auld days as a mute."

"I'm no mute," the Sergeant burst out.

"I meant you look like a mute," I said. "Like you'd follow a hearse in top hat and tails."

"We seem to be getting off topic," the Inspector said. "I asked you if you thought your father had anything to do with the state your mother's in."

Jeez oh, I thought, it's going be a long night.

"Any chance of a cushion," I said. "These chairs are murder. If you're determined to stay on topic, we'd be as well being comfy."

## Miss Ferguson, the Fitter's Daughter.

When I cook I like to roll my sleeves up. I like to do everything by scratch—knead my own pastry, string my own black pudding—and I don't mind making a mess. A couple of years back I realised I might be able to make a living at it, when my pal Allison told me about the evening classes at the college. When I left school at sixteen, I was your typical teenager, bored and clueless. The only things I liked were boys, plays, and cooking. Boys, well, you can guess why I liked boys. Old-fashioned plays I liked 'cause they had a real story in them, with a beginning, a middle, and an end, and you could belt right through one in a couple of hours. As for cooking, it's true we didn't do much in home economics beyond boiled eggs and soldiers, but my yokes always turned out better than anyone else's.

Like I told the Inspector, I've only got one more year

to go till I finish college and then I'll be on my way. Oh, yes—no more '20 Marlborough and a Daily Record, love' for me—I'll be away from the newsagents in Central Station, away from the long shifts, the wise-cracks, the paper cuts.

When the shop's quiet, but, I take the foodie magazines behind the till and copy the recipes into jotters that Allison got for me when she worked at the primary. I've different jotters for different stuff now, like soups or desserts, game or fish. Some Saturdays I let my girls pick a fancy-schmancy recipe with a boat-load of ingredients and we gie it a go. After nipping down to the Co-op for any whats-its I don't have, we line everything up on the kitchen counter. Every pot, pan and ladle, the floor, the cooker and ourselves ends up sticky with stock, spices and peelings. It's a laugh, a carry-on, a family game we've invented. Sometimes we eat the results too, but that's not the point, is it?

"Calm down, hen," I said. The Inspector seemed right anxious to know where my kids were. "They're with their father. Do you think I'd leave them with any-old-body?"

Normally, it's Allison that looks after them while I'm working but, now she's quit the school canteen. Then my sister comes round nights twice a week to let me get to college. Their father doesn't see them that often—most of the time he doesn't bother. Apart from emergencies, he only turns up when he's feeling guilty or horny, or both.

"I can just see him," I said to the Inspector. "He'll be stuffing them with sweeties and then rolling round with them till they boke."

"Thought you were a single parent, Carol-Anne."

"I am," I said. "But I'm no the Virgin Mary. My kids didn't arrive in an Easter egg. "

"But you're not married to this Alec?" The Inspector wore a ring, naturally.

"I'm a modern woman. This Alec and I enjoy a modern relationship. We respect each others' personal space."

"And why's that?"

"No mystery—he drives me round the fucking bend."

"It must be hard," she went on, "raising two on your own."

"Why? I brought them in to the world—they didn't ask to be here. Hell mend you if you can't raise your own weans."

"True—we have to live with our choices."

"Spare me the philosophy, hen. You'll be laughing out the other side of your face when your man slips one past the goalie—and all your pals in blue round here step on your head on their way up the sweet ladder of success."

She threw me a look that could've stripped paint, then threw a second one at his nibs, but he was back hunting for better days in his tie.

My eldest girl had just turned seven, and my youngest was five and a half. Pint-sized terrors—got screams that would frighten the French. Pure gorgeous, like their names. Fairy tales those names—and that's what their lives would be like if I'd anything to do with it.

The Sergeant readjusted his bones in his chair. I wouldn't have been surprised if I'd looked up and seen strings and a hand. "Tatiana and Viola?" he repeated, like he'd tasted something off.

"Just because I work in a shop, Sergeant, doesn't mean I canny read. I've been known to crack a spine, in my time."

"Bet they get the piss taken out them at school," he said.

"They do not." I was riled now.

"Ok, that's enough," the Inspector said.

Or, to be honest, I thought, nothing like what they put up with at home, what with Alec calling Viola, Violin for a while, then Violet, then Parma, then finally settling on V. As for my Da, Tatiana's own Grandda, he christened her Tattie from the get-go, till he decided that Spud was even better.

"What about your parents, Carol-Anne?"

"What about them?"

"You never leave your daughters with them?"

"They're no a baby-sitting service, they've served their time."

"Your sister left her son there today."

"No, she didn't. She left him with me and I took him visiting."

"Really? That's odd, because Archie was seen playing down the back green this afternoon, but your car didn't turn up outside until about fifteen minutes before we arrived. You were in a bit of a rush, apparently, because you bumped the car behind you when you reversed in."

"Well, that's what bumpers are for, Inspector."

I switched my attention to Laurel. My Da always said that no man would tolerate my cheek were it not for my two saving graces—great teeth and great tits.

"May I please have a drink of water, Sergeant?" I said, blessing him with an eye-full of both. He was on his feet in a twinkling and lolloping out the door like a happy giraffe before the Inspector could rope a lasso. She leaned back and sighed.

Today had been a total cluster-fuck, no argument. Sheena had called my cell this afternoon but I'd ignored it 'cause, well, I was distracted. When I got home from work around three-thirty, I took over from Allison, then V and Spud started fighting over DVDs, and then wanted me to watch *Shrek* with them for the billionth time.

I'd planted my rump on the sofa beside them, when my cell rang. I was about to answer it but the door went. Ringing, ringing everywhere—a right Quasimodo moment. I ignored the phone and went to the door and there he was, that glaekit-dough-heed, the girls' father, standing there with his face tripping him, the pints still reflecting in his eyes. Oh, away and play in the traffic, Alec, I said, trying to shut the door again, but he had his great fat foot stuck in it.

Oh, Carol-Anne—then he started—saying my name the way he does when he's pissed, as though its three miles long. Oh, Carol-Aaaaanne, oh I miss you, Carol-Aaaaanne—his eyelids drooped, he hung off the doorframe, like an aff-kilter ape. Oh, Carol-Aaaaanne—I miss the weans.

Well, here's the weans—I told him—opening the door wide—go and get them, if you miss them that bloody much. Does he go? Does he hell. Peeps his head into the living-room and gives them a wee wave. Oh, but Carol-Anne—he said, following me into the kitchen—you're such a good mother—that's why I love you—I've always loved you—I've never loved another bird like I love you.

Aye, and no for the want of trying, I said.

I knew what he was after. 'Cause he gets a leg over a couple a times he thinks he owns the bike. It winds me up but. He always turns up all lovey-dovey if he's had a bonus and a drink. The first time I slept with him he told me he'd been sterilised and I believed him, even though he's Catholic. Then our Spud pops along. You'd think I'd have had more sense, but no, I go and do it again. It's not that he's that great looking—heavy-built, spongy body, ponsy-posh-boy hair, but he has a voice like a Scottish Orson Wells—my best defence is to prevent him from talking. If I give him space for a paragraph, I swear my knickers drop on their own. It was only afterwards that I remembered to check my cell phone messages.

"Did you call my sister?" I said.

"Of course," the Inspector said. "She is the boy's mother."

"Is she here?"

"Don't you worry about that."

"Can I speak to her, but? Because she'll be upset and she's my wee sister, and I'm the one that should tell her what happened."

"What *did* happen, Carol-Anne?"

"I told you, already, nothing happened. My Ma fell over. End of story."

## Miss Ferguson, the Fitter's (other) Daughter.

When I was in fifth year at secondary school and Sheena was in first, I caught her in the girls' bogs, taking a swig from the communal bottle of Vodka that always lived on the window ledge of the far end cubicle. Her and her pals had dogged French and were singing away to "Tinsel Town in the Rain" on the radio, as if they were first to discover the wonders of *The Blue Nile*. I dragged her outside and told her if I nabbed her skipping class or drinking again I'd tan her arse. She said sorry, and okay, and never acted embarrassed to get caught or pissed at being humiliated and that's when I knew I'd always need to look out for her.

And I did. I took her shopping for her first make-up and helped her with her homework. Explained the facts of life to her, too, when the boys starting buzzing around, because I knew my Ma and my Da wouldn't bother, 'cause they never bothered for me, and our Sheena was triple-handicapped—cute, gormless, and gullible. She's still the same, and that's how my Da came up with the game plan. We had to think again, but, when the silly bisum got pregnant and it turned out to be a boy.

Our Sheena, the reason she needed me this afternoon was to look after Archie while she went to track down her man. The penny had finally dropped about his phantom building contracts. For the last few months, he'd been leaving her to go and work in Newcastle because he said the money was better, but she hadn't seen a pound note of difference. Then around four-ish she tries calling me 'cause somebody had seen him outside a motel in Stirling. But, of course, she can't get hold of me, and she's that ditzy she gets in the car and does what I'd told her time and again to never do—she takes our Archie over to his Granny and Grandda's and dumps him there. And all 'cause I didn't answer my phone—yet another shag I'm going to regret for the rest of my life.

"What does your sister's husband do?" the Inspector asked.

"They're no married. He's a builder. I think he's in Newcastle at the moment, but."

"Where do they live?"

"Easterhouse."

The inspector nodded. She had kind eyes. In different circumstances, me and her could have been pals, had a drink the-gether, shared some shit and giggles.

"And I worry about her being there, you know?" I said. "Every time he goes away, he leaves her in that flat and she's scared being in Easterhouse on her own, and I don't blame her—it's the fucking West Bank round there. I mean, I know the council's been trying to smarten it up— Beirut with lipstick now—but they still nick or snort, or blow everything to bits that's no screwed down. Some of the tenements are pitch black with all the windows boarded 'cause there's no a chink of glass left. And I've told her to move herself and Archie in with me and the girls, we've plenty of room, but, oh, no, our Sheena wants her independence. Well, hell mend you, I've told her, if you're lying there alone at night with bullets fleeing past you in the dark and punching pinholes in the wood chip."

"And how old is Archie?"

"Did you no ask him yourselves?"

"I'm asking you."

"He's a fibber, mind."

"Carol-Anne—will you just answer the damn question—how old is he?"

"He's four going on five. Who calls their wean 'Archibald' nowadays, by the way? Archibald. Jesus. You think my girls have it hard? Well, God help him when he starts school. I think that was Rock's idea."

"Rock?"

"As you've gathered by now, Sergeant, we have a tal-

ent for names in our family. It's Rock as in Rock Hudson—
Sheena's man's ma was daft for Rock Hudson. I once told
her that he was Crossmyloof—you know, a poof like—
not our Sheena's Rock—the real one. Well, we know our
Rock isn't—got proof, so to speak—anti-poof-proof—oh,
got a wee smile out of the Inspector there—but his ma
didn't believe a word of it. "

"What's he like, this Rock?"

"Nice enough."

Despite Rock's extra-curricular activities, I'd always
liked him. Unlike Alec who done a bunk as soon as he
knew I was pregnant, Rock stuck around to live with the
fruit of his labours. And he wasn't mean either—never
turned up at your door with both arms the same length—
always brought a little something with him. Usually
something that fell off the back of a lorry—mind you—
but it's the thought that counts—and our Sheena was that
clueless she didn't know that half the stuff lying around
their place was nicked, and I told him, hell mend you,
Rock, I said, if you get caught. But in a way, he was bringing in a wage and Sheena should've married him when
he asked her. And he kept asking her and she kept saying no. Well, hell mend her now, because it looks like
he's woken up and changed horses.

Not that I told the police any of that. Our Sheena. Jeez-
oh, what will we do with her? As minced as she was when
she was twelve. I used to think I was the family ding-bat,
but I see now that she was the odd one out all along,
because she was the only one who didn't know.

Someone knocked the door and the Sergeant got up to
answer it. He came back with a bit of paper and handed
it to the Inspector. She read it then looked at me.

"You were watching Archie, were you?"

I crossed my arms.

"According to your sister, she left her son with your
mother at four this afternoon because she had a family
emergency in Stirling. She tried calling you first but she
couldn't reach you."

The Inspector gave the paper to the Sergeant who didn't know what to do with it. After dithering about for a moment, he rolled it up like a cigarette and stuck it behind his ear.

"By the way, Carol-Anne, where's Billy?"

"Billy? Billy who?"

"Your brother."

## Master Ferguson, the Fitter's Son.

It broke Ma's heart when our Billy left home. Billy was the youngest and there was never any doubt he was the favourite. He was only thirteen when he scarpered, and my Ma hadn't seen hide nor tail of him since. Going on five years now. She staggered around like a zombie for weeks after he left. It was all I could do to get her to nibble a digestive. She kept asking me where her Billy had gone, and I'd say, I don't know, Ma, I don't know. For a while there me and my Da got a bit frantic because she'd pester everyone she met—in the close, in the supermarket, in the post office—have you seen my Billy? We were frightened to leave her on her own in case she hurt herself, but then one day she just stopped talking about him. It was as if she'd worked out that we'd only been trying to do our best for the both of them.

He didn't really have any option, my Da, not after he found out what was going on. And the two of us thegether decided not to tell Sheena, because Sheena's a worrier and canny keep a secret. Da took care of the school and I gave Billy some choices. First he wanted to stay, then he wanted to go. Teary one minute, smirking the next. Our Hamlet couldn't make up his mind. Finally I lost the rag and made it up for him and sent him to stay with one of my old boyfriends who ran a hostel in Liverpool. And he's been there ever since. Fitted right in—said he'll never be back. I send him money, and when I get the chance, nip down to see him. My Da's not been though, it's not that he blames him—he just canny bring himself to go.

"You never reported your brother missing?"
"We did."
"We've no record of it."
I shrugged. "No my fault if you canny file."
"What was he like?"
"Typical teenager. Moody wee shite, always skulking in his room. Met every question with a grunt."
"Where do you think he is?"
"London, probably. Isn't that no where they all end up?"
The Inspector slowly shook her head. I blinked and looked away.
"Miss him, but," I said.

### Ferguson, the Fitter

My Da's been a fitter for Weirs for over forty years. He joined as an apprentice straight out of school when he was fifteen. He can make any tool on the planet and work a lathe with his eyes shut, measuring down to a sixteenth of an inch using only his fingerprints. Has hands as scarred and battered looking as old leather gloves.

He met my Ma through my Ma's brother, my Uncle Harry, who worked alongside Da in the factory. Harry wasn't as good at it as Da though, the quality of my Da's milling and turning soon left Harry in the dust. Da always said he fell in love with Ma at first sight, though I've often wondered if it was love or no something more akin to pity. Her and Harry's parents had died when that ferry went down off the Ayrshire coast way back, and Harry was left to bring her up on his own, and Da always said Harry was a bit of an arsehole and didn't know the first thing about how to raise a wee lassie.

She'd been waiting outside Weir's gates for Harry one day, in her school uniform. Sixteen years old. That's when my Da first saw her. "Pleased to meet you, Mr. Ferguson," she'd said, even though he was only seven years older. She gave him her hand. It was as soft as a daisy petal and her eyes were flecked with gold. These are his very words. Always tells that story the same way—"soft as a daisy petal" and "eyes flecked with gold,"—as if he's learned it by heart, like the Lord's Prayer or the ten-times table. He's still a sad sap. "Put the kettle on, petal," he'll say, or "Hey, flower, where's my Rangers socks?" on the few occasions, now, that is, that he bothers to talk to her.

Da's always loved kids. Since Billy, but, he's had to pretend he doesnay. He's acted like he canny abide them for so long, I'm beginning to think he believes it. He'll no have them in the house. I remember the first time Sheena took our Archie round there, when Archie started to toddle. My Ma had called her from the bingo because she needed a lift home. The woman she normally went with had been carted off to the Southern General for an emergency hernia operation, after collapsing over her numbers.

Sheena had to take Archie with her to pick my Ma up. And she told me that when she brought Ma home, she found Da in the living-room sitting on that old clatty chair of his, with an ashtray on one arm and the telly buttons on the other, stuffing spilling all over the place and ring pulls jammed down the sides. His face was like a burst couch and all. You take that wee shite away from under my feet, he said to Sheena, even though he'd barely seen him. The poor lamb was only standing in the hall picking his nose and drawing imaginary circles on the wallpaper. It worked. He was that rude about Archie, Sheena never took him back. Till today.

I didn't want Da accused of favouritism so I couldn't take my girls round there either. Sometimes, he'd nip over on his way home from work to give them pocket money and a hug. Besotted with them; it breaks his heart that he can't see them more often. Mind you, I don't go round there much myself, it's too depressing. I don't like to see him drunk and my Ma all tensed up like a watch.

"Does your father drink, Carol-Anne," the Inspector

asked.

"Is the Pope a Catholic?"

"I mean more than normal."

"What's normal round here?"

"Where's his local?"

"You're no still looking for him, are you? Don't know why yous are bothering. He's most likely at the Lodge, but, he goes there after the bookies on a Saturday."

"The Lodge," the Inspector smiled.

Yes, well might you smile, Inspector, I thought, you weren't there when I told my Da about Alec. Alec wouldn't have been Da's first choice to father his grandchildren, let's put it that way. My father lacks affection for left-footers. He's in all the marches—fancies his-self a right Billy Boy. That's why my wee brother was named Billy. In honour of. I once told my Da King William was a poof, but he was having none of it.

"If you ask him nice, Serg," I said, "He'll teach you the funny handshake. You'll no get far in this profession without knowing that Masonic tickle."

"Does he have any other bad habits?"

"Bad habits? What do you mean? Since when has being a Proddy been a bad habit? What's our Archie been saying?"

"I'm asking you if your father was ever violent."

"That's what you're asking, is it? You must think I came up the Clyde in a banana-boat. You's have all got minds like sewers, so you's have. Well, my Da isn't like that. He's a bloody saint, you've no idea."

Not like Uncle Harry. I could have told them some tales about him. Mind you, Uncle Harry didn't get away with it with me—I knew better by then—I was fly for it—would have knocked him into the middle of next week if he'd tried. Go away and play with yourself, you dirty bugger, I said to him once. But Harry's dead now—been dead for yonks.

**Mistress Ferguson, the Fitter's Wife**.

She's had it hard, my Ma. She's like a skivvy. I've told

her—you're like a skivvy, I've said—you don't need to whitewash the stairs every month—steeping sheets in the bath—ironing the towels. The days for all that shite are long passed. But she wouldn't listen. Never says much either—no a great one for the conversation.

She was a good mother to us, though, to me and Sheena. Clean school uniforms, three meals a day. Gentle, mousey, bit of a doormat, right enough, to teenage girls, so Da was the one that kept us in line. Her and my Da—I watched them sometimes—like two goldfish in a bowl—swimming round and round each other and barely a word. All politeness, but no even a kiss at Christmas. He still called her "flower" and "petal," but I doubt he'd laid a finger on her for years.

Must be right lonely for her, I thought. And she scurries after him like a serf. I think she thinks she owes him. Maybe so, but there's a limit. I offered to take her in. Come and stay with me, Ma, I said. Oh no, she said, I'll no be allowed to do that. I'll speak to him, I told her, don't you worry. But no, the stupid cow stayed. I was fuming—that's gratitude for you. Well, hell mend her, it's her funeral. Feeling sorry day-in-day-out is no way to live.

"I'm concerned about Archie," the Inspector said.

My heart sank to my Ma's sandals. Two sets of eyes on me as I plucked at fluff on my Da's cardigan.

"He won't speak to anyone, including his mother."

"That's no odd," I said, looking up, relieved. "He's another moody wee sod—takes after our Billy that way."

"Yes, but he seems exceptionally withdrawn."

"You'd be withdrawn if you'd seen your Granny break her nose. He'll be fine, no worries. I'll talk to him. Our family takes care of our own."

"Why don't you take another stab at telling me what happened?"

"You really need to get that short-term memory loss seen to."

"Sergeant MacIntyre's going to write it down this time, till I get a chance to my head examined," she said, in a snotty tone.

"Fine, then. Sharpen your pencil, sunshine, and keep up."

If the Inspector was telling me the truth it meant Archie had kept his side of the bargain.

"You're right, I wasn't looking after Archie. I was supposed to have been and I feel bad about that, but something came up. Anyways, I went to my Ma and Da's around half-four to pick up the Next catalogue, and when I got there my Ma was giving Archie a bath. The floor was slidey. She lost her balance and fell into the medicine cabinet and smashed her nose. Made a right racket, glass everywhere. I was mopping her up when you lot all charged in like the cavalry."

The Sergeant finished taking notes and rested his pen on the table. The Inspector looked at me, with her arms crossed and her head tilted to one side like it was too heavy for her neck. I wrapped my Da's cardigan tighter around my middle and folded my arms.

"Is this going to take much longer?" I said. "I swear I can feel the menopause coming on."

Nobody said anything; you could have heard a nit sneeze. The Sergeant doodling, the Inspector watching me, and me keeping my tongue clamped, tight, between my teeth.

## Happy Families

It had been a dull day, and round about four the sky was already purpling behind the bedroom blinds. The window was open, and the air tasted like metal. The music over the credits for *Shrek* muffled through the wall from the living-room next door. I sat on the edge of the bed and checked my messages. The tone of Sheena's voice told me before I'd even finished listening that she'd gone and done something stupid. I yanked clothes on and left

Alec fumbling for his trousers. I told him to keep an eye on the girls, that I'd be back in a tick.

I drove like Dario over to my parents' flat, circling the tenement twice because I couldn't find anywhere to park, before chancing a toty wee space at the front. I thought I'd hit something, but I never bothered checking because my guts were churning.

Mrs. MacGregor stood at the entrance to the close. Silly cow thinks she's living in Balmoral. The only flat in the tenement with a red door—the rest of them manage to make-do with corporation green. Got enough flowers in pots on her front step to fill the Blue Peter garden. Neds keep nicking them but she just puts out more. She's like a charity.

"Oh, excuse me, love," she said, wearing gardening gloves like Martha fucking Stewart, and putting out her arm to stop me running up the stairs. "I think maybe your father needs a wee hand." Then she minces away right pleased with herself.

Well, I couldn't find him to start with because he was round the back green—sitting on the damp grass under the whirligig singing to himself. "Daisy, Daisy, give me your answer do…" Jesus—he was absolutely paralytic. Steaming. "Oh, here's my lovely lassie," he said, opening his arms. "To gie her Da a hand."

I managed to get him on his feet, then up the stairs— he weighed a ton and he'd medlayed into some smutty jingle about the Pope—and I wish he'd shut up because that nosy cow's front door's twitching, and I dreaded the other neighbours coming out to enjoy the free show. He told me all about his afternoon, all about his win on the horses, all about the dominoes at the Lodge.

No-one answered the bell, so I took out my spare keys and we went inside. I propped my Da against the hall table and caught my breath. The flat felt too quiet.

"Ma?" I said, and headed down to the kitchen. I turned back toward the bathroom. I'd heard voices and a splash.

Da got there before me. He shoved the door open with

his shoulder. I ran up behind him. Ma was standing in her dressing gown, looking down into the tub at Archie, who had his knees pulled up to his chest, squished in the corner by the taps. His cheeks were flushed, oily. Playing cards were spread across the floor. Ma stepped away when she saw my Da, and pulled her hands into fists then put them behind her back.

"What you doing, petal?" Da said. He'd sobered up smartish.

She stood there, staring at him, like a fart in a trance.

"I'm sorry," she said. She looked down at Archie, then back at my Da. "I didn't mean to…It's…we were playing a wee game."

Da swayed back like a comic drunk, then snapped forward and head-butted her in the face. Her nose burst like a pomegranate, and she fell smack into the medicine cabinet, sending glass whistling and javelin over the washbasin and the floor. Archie opened his mouth and yowled like a trapped cat.

I grabbed Da by the back of his jacket, then by the arse of his trousers, to stop him from belting her again, hauled him around, and threw him out the bathroom, locking the door behind him. Ma slithered down the wall and sat on her bum, the blood pooling in her lap. Her dressing-gown was all hitched up; she was naked underneath. I made her decent, tightened its cord.

"I'm sorry, I'm sorry," she kept saying.

"Don't worry, Ma," I told her. "Shhh… ssshh." I needed her to shut up. "It's no your fault—the big drunken eejit's off his head."

I shunted her away from the wall, tilted her head back and stuck a towel under her nose. The wean was still bawling. "Clamp it, Archie, will you?" I said, "It's ok."

I plucked him out the tub and pulled the plug, and wrapped him in a towel. Still bawling. "Oh, for heaven's sake, son, gie us peace." I said. "Now, stand there and don't move."

Da was out in the hall, kneeling down on one knee with

a hand on the telephone table like he was taking confession, greetin' and saying it's his fault. I'd just sat down beside him when we both heard someone rapping on the front door. We looked at each other and held our breathes.

"Oh, Mrs. Ferguson? Are you alright? It's me, Mary McGregor from downstairs, is everything ok?"

We waited, kneeling on the floor, clutching onto one another. We must have looked fucking stupid. Both of us feart to move – like the Franks and the Gestapo. She chapped the door again, then, eventually, we heard her goose-stepping away.

"It's my fault," Da started again.

"Aye, so it bloody will be," I said, "If you don't get out of here before either me or the police give you a swift kick up the arse."

I told him to bugger off, I'd deal with it, pulling him to his feet for the second time that day, and not to come back till he'd sobered up. He staggered out the door, blubbering.

I went back into the bathroom with clothes for Archie. Dressing him was tough because he was wet and squirming.

"Archie, will you be done with the wailing?"

The veins in his neck jangled like cords. His nose was coated in snot. He took a deep breath, winding himself up like a siren to start again.

"Enough!" I shook him hard. The shock surprised him. I grabbed his head between my palms.

"Look at me," I said. He tried to turn his face away, but I forced it back.

"Look at me. Now listen—you know that scooter you told me you wanted?"

A sneaky glint came into his eyes.

"If you promise not to talk to a single other person till I tell you, I'll get it for you, ok?"

He gulped, then his eyes squeezed into skinny slits and I knew I had him.

"Now, I mean no-one, Archie. No even your Ma."

He nodded. The sneaky glint was still there. I'd seen a look like that once before, the day I put our Billy on the train to Liverpool.

Ma still sat with her head back, whispering to the ceiling, dabbing at her nose with the towel. It was when I'd started gathering up the cards that I heard the me-maws screeching to a halt at the bottom of the close, then the Doc Martins pummelling up the stairs.

## Game Plan

You'd have thought the three of us were in church, we had been that quiet for so long. It was almost a shock when a policewoman came through the interview room door. It was the one who'd taken Archie away. She whispered something in the Inspector's ear.

"Oh, for Christ's sake," the Inspector said. The policewoman left. "It appears your father turned up at the hospital and apologised to your mother."

I shut my eyes, and sighed. Our move of last resort— Da taking the rap. We'd agreed he'd take the rap for all of it, if things ever got that far.

"Why couldn't you tell me, Carol-Anne? When I asked you over an hour ago if he was ever violent, and saved us all this bother?"

"I'm no a snitch."

"What a bloody waste of my time!" The Inspector stood up and shoved her chair under the table. "She's not pressing charges, so you can go."

"All this fuss over a whack." I could barely keep the relief out my voice. "If Mrs. McG. hadn't been such a quick-draw McGraw with the phone—this would have blown over. This is what happens when people don't mind their own business."

The Inspector went to the door, opened it, and turned around. "Your father's here, by the way," she said. "He's outside. Your mother too. In fact, your whole damn clan is outside."

She still held the door open. "Did you hear me, Carol-Anne? I said you could go."

"I heard you." I tried to stand up but my legs felt like pastry. "Just give us a minute," I said. "I need a minute."

# The End of the Season

SHE REQUESTED THAT THE VISITOR be shown into the drawing room, while she finished a letter. After tidying her writing desk, she patted her gray hair and smoothed the front of her stiff black gown before heading downstairs.

Had Mrs. Charles Merrick been willing to examine her feelings, she would have realized that she had been expecting this visit, and that she was relieved, relieved in the way that someone gravely ill must be relieved to know that one is, in fact, dying, and that suffering from uncertainty has ceased.

In the drawing room, cream linen shades blotted the thick New York summer. At first Mrs. Merrick could not see her, because her visitor skulked in a corner where shadows clustered as though ashamed. Then the woman startled as if she had been caught doing something uncouth. Her hands were fisted over the porcelain handle of a fragile parasol.

"Why, Miss Parker," said Mrs. Merrick. "Sarah, my dear."

Mrs. Merrick beckoned the younger woman toward her. Miss Parker hesitated momentarily then succumbed. Their bustles crackled like kindling as they wove, hand-linked and cautious, between spindly tables to stiff chairs before an unlit fire.

Miss Parker's face was flushed. Perhaps it was the heat, perhaps the flurry of her hansom cab ride, trying to protect the pale lemon silk from smudges or her brown eyes from being caught by the glance of a stranger, or perhaps it was the daring of her enterprise, for a single young lady traveling alone outside of the acceptable calling hours was apt to stain more than a dress.

"Mrs. Merrick," she began, "I didn't mean to disturb you." She perched on the edge of the chair. Unsure where to put her parasol, she propped it against a side table, her hand hovering in front of it as if it, or she, might fall. "Whatever must you think of me?"

"I don't know what to think of you, my dear," Mrs. Merrick replied. "As I've yet to discover why you are here." This remark was naked of the customary obliqueness but adorned by Mrs. Merrick's high smile. Miss Parker paused as though scolded. Mrs. Merrick leaned forward, causing her bodice to creak.

"It's always a pleasure to see you," she said, "Nevertheless."

The room was comfortable and ornamented with trumpet lilies and Chinese vases, Russian lacquer boxes and Baedekers, all the accumulated bric-a-brac of Mrs. Charles Merrick's celebrated stylishness. Miss Parker, however, ignored the trinkets around her and concentrated on arranging her dress, as if gathering her thoughts in its folds.

Mrs. Merrick watched the young woman's tentative steps toward the hazardous waters of conversation and decided to plunge in ahead.

"I should have moved on to Newport, you know," she said, "now the season is over." She fingered the jet strands at her neck. "It is only by good fortune that you caught me."

She waited patiently. No, a little impatiently—for the other woman to leave shore. Miss Parker appeared unwilling to join her. "Are you in any trouble, my dear?"

Miss Parker shook her head vehemently, then drew a

breath and leapt in. "I wanted to offer my condolences," she said, "on the death of Mr. Merrick's father."

Mrs. Merrick glanced sideways at the marble mantelpiece where the more conventional condolences were arrayed, elegantly scripted and messenger-delivered, trimmed in black ribbon and devoid of the awkwardness of authorial accompaniment. Her gaze slipped back to Miss Parker, who smiled—a smile too broad for elegance, though one had to concede that her teeth were good.

"My husband is at his business premises this afternoon," said Mrs. Merrick. "Something or other about the railway." She twitched her shoulders to indicate her indifference to those masculine concerns. "Normally he is home at this time."

"I know," said Miss Parker.

*I know* she said. Not *Is he?* or *I see,* but *I know.* It was enough. At last, Mrs. Merrick, too, knew. She knew, at last, who and what she was dealing with and the anguish of searching through her broad circle of acquaintances and along the broad avenues of upper Manhattan was over. She felt relief, relief flavored with hard, black anger.

She looked at Miss Parker's face, at the attempt to hide fear and perplexity behind a rosy insouciance, and her mind sailed back over thirty years of other young women fluttering like moths on other sofas and armchairs in New York, Rhode Island or Bar Harbor, young women who had shared that same youthful vitality along with that same naïve expression until the sudden comprehension of the rules of the society in which they lived had passed over their faces like night, for Mrs. Merrick had often felt obliged to inform them of the bleaker realities, the unbearable demands of loyalty, the stultifying disease of boredom, and the slippery nature of reputation, obliged because her husband walked through their dark world like light, and as she pondered her choices, entrapment or release, Miss Parker trembled in front of her, flimsy and yellow, on the starched Austrian brocade, and she realized, with a slight surprise, that she wanted to tell this particular young woman to leave. It would be the kindest thing to do. But why be any kinder than had she had been to all the rest?

"You must stay until my husband comes home," said Mrs. Merrick. "You will keep me company."

Miss Parker blinked.

Mrs. Merrick waited in vain for a flurry of excuses, for surely the young woman would flee? She would flutter and bat against the window shades, the picture rails, and cornicing, hurl dizzily beneath the Tiffany glass. All the expensive bric-a-brac would be vulnerable to her attempt. Instead she sat silent, forcing Mrs. Merrick to deal with the repercussions of her choice. Mrs. Merrick leaned over and pulled the crimson bell rope by the fireside. "You know my husband was a great admirer of your father," she said.

An unfortunate subject but the first that came to mind. Charles Merrick and Fitzgerald Parker had gone into business together many years before, but Charles had succeeded where Fitzgerald had failed, as Fitzgerald had been kind but foolish. Since then Fitzgerald Parker had died leaving Sarah Parker and her mother to begin their descent from respectable society, slowly dispensing the last of his income and unable to work or claim kinship with any of the old New York families, as they were Illinois born.

A maid appeared in the doorway.

"We shall have some tea, please, Rosie," said Mrs. Merrick. She turned to her guest, who gazed at her hands on her lap. "No—I think some tea for me and some lemonade for Miss Parker." The young woman glanced up. "You look at little flushed, my dear."

The maid's skirts could be heard sweeping down the hallway. Outside the long windows a few carriages trundled by, the dense air muffling hooves and wheels like eiderdown. Mrs. Merrick sifted through various topics to keep the conversation afloat.

"Are you and your mother still living in that charming little house on 14<sup>th</sup> Street?"

"Yes."

The brownstone was tethered to the stern of the fashionable neighborhoods like a small launch. As more waves of immigrants arrived and society moved farther uptown, Mrs. Merrick knew that the brownstone and its occupants would eventually be cast adrift.

"And I understand you were in the whirl of the season." Mrs. Merrick was swimming resolutely now. "Though, if I may, I'd like to offer a little advice and say you must be more careful about which invitations you accept."

She suspected that Miss Parker was used to advice. Mr. Merrick had always been very free with it. Miss Parker had probably attended many of the best society events, or maybe not the best for she was young and how was she to know, but Mr. Merrick would certainly have secured her invitations to those functions where he might enjoy her company. Mrs. Merrick, so familiar with her husband's machinations, had convinced herself that it was the boring predictability of his deceit that provoked the greatest bitterness, rather than the fact of it.

"And," Mrs. Merrick concluded with another high smile—as though this were the solution to everything— "we must find you a good husband, my dear."

Mrs. Merrick was denied the pleasure of a response by the entrance of the maid carrying a tray bearing tea and a pitcher of lemonade. The maid placed it on a table between them. Mrs. Merrick poured lemonade into a glass and handed it to Miss Parker. It was opaque yet tangy, like sunlight without heat, and Miss Parker gulped it down, spilling a little on her dress. Mrs. Merrick kindly averted her gaze.

The French clock kept languid but remorseless time, while Mrs. Merrick persevered. She talked of art exhibitions and charity events and considered the merits of various respectable bachelors between the ages of twenty-five and fifty, dismissing or approving each in turn until eventually her words dribbled to drops like the dregs at the end of a glass and the two women sat drained and oddly becalmed.

The front door slammed in the hall. Miss Parker flinched and put her glass on the tray with a clatter. Mrs. Merrick remained where she was, one hand under her saucer, the other hanging limp over the side of her chair. The room had darkened so much during their strange vigil that Mrs. Merrick's mourning dress had receded into the shadows and she sensed her resemblance to the Rembrandt that hung on the wall behind her, all ash and pale skin, indefinable outlines and inscrutability. She regreted her decision.

Footsteps echoed in the hall. An exchange of voices. Somewhere, a door closed. Mrs. Merrick pulled the crimson rope.

"Please tell Mr. Merrick to come to the drawing room," she said, when the maid arrived. "I have a surprise for him." She tilted her head toward Miss Parker. "He'll be so pleased to see you."

Miss Parker's hand hovered to one side as if reassuring herself of the location of her parasol. Her eyes were damp and blank.

Mrs. Merrick composed her features, rehearsing her lines for the coming charade. She studied the woman pinned to the chair opposite her, at the yellow satin ribbon binding the young thin neck and felt her resolution falter. Miss Parker's pulse beat rapidly beneath the freckles of her modest décolletage and the rosy glow had faded from her cheeks, leaving the tip of her nose bright red. Mrs. Merrick wanted to say something but she was so used to not saying what she meant that the demands of truth seemed beyond her.

"Miss Parker," she said. She paused, looked at the empty hearth, tugged at the cuffs of her gown and began again.

"Sarah," she said. "Although my husband is generous with his affections, his memory is short and it would be unfair of me, or anyone else, to demand too much from him." The honey particles of dust swirling in front of the window shades appeared to buoy her words up in the air. "I do hope, my dear, you have not been so foolish as to have believed everything he said."

Miss Parker's hands flew to cover her face. Mrs. Merrick stretched across the tea table and caught them in her own. Waves of comprehension and sympathy washed over the two women and they clung to one another, speechless, to save themselves from drowning.

The drawing room door opened. Miss Parker emitted a slight gasp, dropped Mrs. Merrick's hands, and sprang to her feet. Her bustle clipped the tray and toppled a sugar bowl to the floor. It bounced, unheeded, on the Oriental rug in a soft billow of crystals.

Charles Merrick stood in the doorway, his expression impassive, and one hand resting on his necktie. At the sight of her handsome husband, Mrs. Merrick pulled back from the truth and straightened her spine. A resigned smile played lightly on his lips, as he briefly acknowledged Miss Parker's presence with a swift nod in her direction without taking his eyes from his wife's face. Then he slipped his other hand into a trouser pocket and jingled some coins, like a gambler who has just lost a round of cards but is calculating whether he has enough left to risk another bet.

This gesture streamed over Mrs. Merrick like cold water and she saw him, as if for the first time. She noted the casual elegance of his stance, the complacent confidence in his wrinkled yet boyish face, and his complete disregard for the pretty prey that stood quivering between them, and she knew he was relying on her to finish the game with the same innate sense of propriety she had shown in the past.

She rose and slipped one arm around the young woman's slim waist.

"Is it not astonishing, Charles," she said, "that Miss Parker should cross New York, all alone, and on such a day, just to call on people like us?"

# Slipping the Moorings

I HAD TAKEN A WRONG ROAD somewhere. The scenery appeared unfamiliar and it shouldn't have been; I grew up in this part of the country. Surely I hadn't forgotten everything?

"Slow down," said Annie. She turned and smiled at Lauren and Jacob sitting in the back. "Feels like the Indy 500, doesn't it?"

The dearth of signs didn't help. I knew I could drive around the Isle of Mull's periphery in either direction and we'd still reach Tobermory, but it was a long way for a short cut and we'd miss the ferry. It was Iona's fault for talking me into this hare-brained trip. After my mother's funeral five years before, I swore I'd never come back.

The sea ebbed on our left, the landscape rippled away on our right, whitewashed cottages with dark roofs and windows scattered like dice in its tousled green folds.

"Told you we should have brought the Tom-Tom," Annie said, reaching for the map.

"I don't need a navigation system to find my way home."

We'd spent the first four days of our visit to Scotland at my sister's house in Glasgow, in its matchy-matchy bedrooms with the sparsely-populated shelves. Annie adapted easily to the smaller space, she can adapt to pretty much anything, and even our normally ramshackle off-spring seemed cowed by the petite and immaculate surroundings, so different from our sprawling, cluttered bungalow on the outskirts of Berkley.

Lauren and Jacob folded in their arms and legs like Swiss army-knives and tucked themselves into pockets of their Aunt Iona's furniture. I was proud of them, of their "pleases" and "thank-you's," of their managing to hold their tongues despite their bemusement over everyone having to share a single bathroom, despite their Aunt's wobbly interpretation of Lauren's vegetarianism. Nevertheless, any pretence that this was a holiday, with jaunts to the art gallery and the transport museum, was shattered by my sister's persistent hectoring.

"You'll just have to tell him," Iona repeated, the night before we left to drive north. "He won't listen to me."

"I will, I will."

"It's all right for you. You're well out the way of it. I'm the one that's fleeing up and down that bloody A82 with broth every other weekend like a blue-arsed fly."

"Yes, I realize that..."

"And don't *ask* him—it's not a quiz—*tell* him."

"I know, I know."

"Selfish bugger, so he is. Still living in the back-end of beyond."

"It's home, though."

"Oh, it is, is it? I guess if you've nothing to do but pick your nose and look out the window, Angus, you can afford to be sentimental—but some of us have lives."

We missed the three o-clock ferry. After a wander around Tobermory's gaudy-colored harbor and a visit to the distillery, we caught the next boat at five. On the Ardnamurchan peninsula, the road narrowed to a single track through gray hills shrubby with bracken and purple with broom, bordered by disheveled stone walls. The coastline beyond Kilchoan writhed and twisted, stumbling toward the Hebridean Sea.

The afternoon waned yet the sun remained high; the distance between crofts increased. My mood, temporarily soothed in Tobermory, began to thrum again at the approach of recognizable landmarks. I pointed these out to Annie and the kids—the only tree worth climbing for at least fifteen miles, the steep yet shallow Sanna burn where I'd hurtled down on my bike to skinned-knee disaster, the secret arc of Portuairk bay with its sliver of perfect yellow sand. This last site required me to stop and park the car. Long after they'd all piled back in, I stood looking down at the water until Annie shouted, "Let's go!"

Twenty minutes later we drove into the rutted remains of my father's garden. I imagined him, in his old tufted armchair, watching us through the bottle-glass windows of the cottage's living room, and sensed his satisfaction as our wheels slotted into the grooves of the neglected lawn. I turned off the engine. Lauren sighed behind me, my daughter's bewilderment evident despite her attempt to maintain an air of worldliness.

Annie folded the map. "Iona was right," she said. "It is the back-end of beyond."

She opened her door. I stayed where I was.

"Bet you ten bucks he asks if we got lost," I said.

My wife is the life raft in our family; we rely on her to keep us afloat when the rest of us tire of swimming. I know how selfish that sounds, but we all slip into roles, and that was the role that she, and we, had chosen for her. She would be my ally against the wiliness of my father, and although I appreciated the support I knew it wouldn't be enough.

I saw him. He had paused on the threshold of the cottage to tuck the tails of his shirt into old corduroys. The children got out and leaned against the car. Lauren had been too young to remember meeting her grandfather at her Aunt Iona's years before, and Jacob didn't know him at all. Normally, I peeled my six-year-old son off strangers like a stray thread, but he eyed his grandfather with uncharacteristic reticence. Meanwhile Lauren's ruthless gaze took in the unkempt salt and pepper beard, the frayed leather belt, and the darned Arran cardigan.

"Did ye get lost," my father said, as I got out the car.

"No," said Annie. "We took the scenic route." Her pronunciation of "route" rhymed with "doubt."

"You yanks fighting again, blondie?" My father hadn't moved from the doorway, one hand clutching the top of the frame as though holding the croft upright.

"If we were, pops," she replied, "You know we'd kick your butts."

He laughed and stepped forward to hug her. Annie's hesitation was so slight, I'm sure only I noticed it. She'd met my father but twice before, both times at Iona's in Glasgow. His disapproval over my choice of an American wife, ("A local girl was good enough for me," he'd said), had been painfully obvious to everyone, though Annie never mentioned it. Another reason why I loved her so much, another reason to avoid coming home.

"Hi," Jacob said, unsure whether to rush and hug, or wait for my signal. I couldn't make that decision for him, so I opened the boot, cutting him from sight.

I carried the bags into the cottage and left Annie to guide the children through their hellos. I intended to delay their entry until I could see if the housekeeping had deteriorated as much as Iona had warned.

It was worse. My mother had always kept the old-fashioned furnishings in meticulous condition, but I found the red velvet curtains sagging, the paisley chenille sofa pummeled beyond resuscitation, and the inherited Afghan parlor rug sticky underfoot. My mother's pride and joy, the hideous oversized dresser that once displayed her willow pattern wedding china, was empty apart from piles of mail and spent matches. The china had been bequeathed to Iona who had promptly boxed it—she'd no intention, she told me, of spending the rest of her life dusting.

I paused, momentarily at a loss. Recent photographs

of Lauren and Jacob sat on the mantelpiece, clumsily mounted in cheap frames. Annie sent pictures to the grandparents of every milestone in our kids' short lives, but I never conceived of my father favoring them more than a passing glance. He hadn't tolerated photographs in the house when Iona and I were young, believing them to be a sign of vanity. I turned away, and opened the windows to freshen air stale with pipe smoke and damp wool.

I got back outside in time to hear Lauren ask my father how he got to the mall, confirming, I thought, his assumptions about the singular cosseting of the American child. I shoved my hands in my pockets and stifled a grimace as he examined my kids, with their perfect teeth, brand name clothes, un-scuffed shoes and covered knees, and pockets bulging with techy paraphernalia. He transferred his gaze from their small blond heads to me—his dark-haired, freckly son—as if doubting their paternity.

Tugging Jacob behind her, Lauren entered the cottage, pausing under the arch of her grandfather's arm.

"It wasn't, like, a trick question," she said. "It was just a joke." Then she lifted herself onto her toes and kissed him. He sprang upright with a start and banged his head on the doorframe.

The answer, of course, was that you didn't get to the mall—not without a long car journey and a ferry crossing, all contingent on the clemency of the weather. Which is why we had brought provisions with us for our week's stay, but when I opened the fridge it bulged with a mishmash of treats—some in faded boxes with expired sell-by dates, probably from the foosty little grocery in Kilchoan.

After a late tea of Marks and Spencer's ham sandwiches and chocolate cake, Annie took the children exploring, leaving my father and me alone in the kitchen. I placed a bottle of whisky on the table.

"I brought you some Tobermory," I said.

"So I see." He lifted the used plates and put them in the sink. "Did you think I couldn't feed you?" He plunged his hands in the water.

"No—I just thought it would be easier." I lifted a tea towel and began to dry the dishes—a family of mismatched crockery and brown Pyrex from the cigarette coupon catalogue—and examined him from behind. He'd become thin, almost reedy, the shoulder seams of his cardigan lay partway down his arms, the sleeve cuffs turned back to keep them dry.

Outside the window, Annie stood haloed against the moist sun, her apple-green waterproof reduced to black. Lauren drifted along, already looking bored. Jacob bounced from rock to rock and disappeared over the incline to the beach. Annie waited until Lauren caught up then paused considering her next move, trying to keep her new boots dry, I thought, even though they were bought specifically to save her feet from getting wet. She hesitated, marooned by tangled bracken and marshy pools. I resisted an impulse to go and rescue her.

"I know why you're here." My father threw cutlery on the draining board. "But I'm no moving."

"That's not why I'm here." We looked at each other. We both knew I lied. "Jacob wanted to meet you. And Annie and Lauren haven't seen you for ages."

"And how old is the lassie, now?"

"Eleven. No, twelve."

"My, my, time flies."

Yes, it does, I wanted to say, yes, it does. It had been difficult to find time to come home, as there was the new company to think about—you don't take leave from a start-up—and then Jacob came along, planned for, of course, but it was a delicate pregnancy, then the move from the coast to the Valley, and then the move from the Valley to Berkley, then the market collapsed and everyone scrambled, including us, but we survived, and then the kids changed schools and wanted to spend holidays at camps (soccer, lacrosse, Spanish), and then there was my wife's family, hordes of them, all living close by and visiting them seemed a better use of time, killing more birds with one stone so to speak and then, of course, there was the small fact that he and I had never got along, and finally, thank God, there was Iona, a rock, and I knew I could rely on her to keep an eye on them (him and my mother) and then just him, and so I had and she had. It's true I had relied on her to deal with all of it, I realized that now, but she never complained. Not at first.

My father attacked the inside of a festering casserole dish with steel wool. We hadn't used a casserole dish at tea.

"Dad," I began.

"You know I can't abide your sister's husband—or Glasgow. And I'm no coming with you either." He jerked his head toward the west where the waterlogged sun puddled into the sea. "I'm no going o'er there."

"I know that, and I'd never ask you."

"Just make sure you don't."

I drew breath and looked out the window again. Annie and the kids had disappeared. I cradled the dripping, half-dirty casserole in my arms.

"Iona's new place seems comfortable," I persisted, trying to gauge his mood from his profile. "Right next door to Andrew's practice. Roomy now the boys are at University. Handy for the pub. And a nice yard."

"A *yard*? Do you no mean a garden? Christ's sake, you even sound like them now."

"Them? Who's them, Dad? My wife and your grandchildren?"

"Oh, dry your eyes. I'm only pulling your leg."

"Here," I handed him the casserole. "You'll need to give this another go, you made a right balls-up of it the first time."

I folded the dishtowel and placed it on the draining board. My father concentrated on scrubbing out the remnants of whatever crap still lined the dish.

During weekly (no, perhaps monthly), telephone calls

home, I tried to map out our conversations in advance to avoid words like "garbage," "cookies," or "vacation," those audible tidbits of treason, knowing he lay ready to ambush such evidence of my betrayal.

I was the last in a long line of cultural adulterers. Like his brothers, my uncles, I had been born in one country, but lived in and loved another. Even if I wanted to come back, I knew I couldn't, not as long as he was alive, because I'd have to endure his crowing conviction that he'd been right, and that here was where we all fit best. His brothers had left Scotland for anywhere with a cheap passage and the chance of work. They had promised to return if, and when, fortunes were made. My father looked after his parents and eked out a living off the land. But his brothers never came back, and he refused to leave, and he never forgave them for their desertion. He reveled in third-hand tales of their failure. And I was the ultimate traitor of all. Not only had I deserted, I had failed to fail, or at least I'd kept my failures secret from him; indeed I'd told him nothing but good of America, exaggerating my professional successes, smoothing over the bumps in my adopted lifestyle, knowing as I did, with a kind of perverse delight, that he couldn't tolerate comparisons with any other way of life, frightened they may prove to be true.

"Anyway," he dried his hands. "You'll come home eventually."

"The kids are American."

"They'd settle down fast enough."

"And Annie and I? What would we do, exactly?" He didn't reply. "Home is wherever they are."

"No," he said. "Home is where you're born."

The telephone rang in the living room. He disappeared, returning a moment later.

"It's your sister. You can tell her I'm no senile yet."

I went into the living room and lifted the receiver.

"Well, have you sorted it out?"

"Give me a chance, Iona," I whispered, "I've only just

got here." Flummoxed by the accuracy of that statement, she harrumphed loudly before re-hashing the speech she'd given repeatedly in Glasgow.

While she barreled along, I re-calculated in my head whether I could advance Iona whatever money she needed to add the extension to her house for Dad, without either having to sell the croft or Annie having to know. It wouldn't solve the issue of his refusal to move, yet it would be a step in the right direction. But, nope, it didn't matter how I juggled it, I couldn't afford it. My first company had collapsed and my second was in start up mode, eating cash, not making it. We lived comfortably, it's true, but on Annie's income, not mine.

I joined Annie on the beach. We linked arms and walked along the shore, watching a pale blue sky mingle into lilac at the horizon. It seemed to me that the pebbles, the seaweed, the lanky strips of defeated clouds, even the tide, held their breath, trying to arrest the decline of the day.

"You told me it always rained," she said.

"Give it half an hour—it will."

"The power of positive thinking."

I assumed she was being ironic. I didn't bother to correct her. Often I found the monotony of California's sunshine beyond tolerance.

"How much of it belongs to your Dad?"

"Almost all of it," I said. "Along the coastline in both directions and back to the main road before we turned in."

"And the tenants?"

"Over that incline. You can't see them from here."

After retiring from harvesting peat, my father survived by renting some of his land to a company that built and maintained holiday cottages.

"Is it worth much?"

"Didn't used to be, but the Highlands are trendy now, so, yeh, it's worth a fair bit."

"I'm glad—for Iona's sake. We don't need it."

"No," I said. "We don't need it."

"Aren't we lucky?" She squeezed my arm.

"Yes, I guess we are."

At the end of the beach, I paused before a steep track leading up from our left and onto the main road.

"Oh, is this it?" Annie said. "Is this where it happened?"

So I told her again about the day they came to take my mother's piano. How I had clung to my mother's legs in the pouring rain, the bubbly seersucker of her apron balled in my fist, and watched three men load it onto the back of an empty milk lorry. They strapped it down with rope. Once secured, two of the men climbed inside the lorry, while the third walked behind, his hand resting on the rump of the old upright piano as if that would be sufficient to halt its thunderous descent should it decide to slip its moorings. Rainwater gushed in rivulets across its tilted keyboard and plunged off the other end. Unprotected by a tarpaulin or a blanket, a detail that hadn't seemed strange to me at the time but appeared so discordant now, the piano climbed this treacherous incline onto the road around the peninsula and then off to who knows where.

"He hadn't wanted her to have it," I said. "What a terrible thing to do."

"Yes, it was," she said. "Perhaps he had his reasons."

"What possible reason could there be?"

Our arms slipped apart. She stuck her hands in the pockets of her anorak and shrugged.

"I don't know, honey, I'm just saying."


The high summer gloaming dripped into inky darkness. I lit the lamps while Annie, Lauren, and Jacob slumped together on the old sofa and endured my father's new-found passion for conversation. With uncharacteristic curiosity he persisted with questions about their life. I tried to suppress a pathetic yearning (which may have had something to do with the open bottle of Tobermory by my side—if the old sod wasn't going to drink it, I would), for it to be *my* turn, for him to ask what I had wanted to be when I was a child (a long distance lorry driver), and about what I had become (a software engineer), and whether or not I was happy.

"A spaceman," Jacob replied.

"Nonsense."

"He'll make a wonderful spaceman," said Annie, catching Jacob's chin and kissing him.

My father turned to Lauren. "And what about you, missy?"

"I want to save the whales."

"From what?"

"Lauren's going to be a great environmentalist," said Annie. "Aren't you, sweet pea?"

"And you're a school teacher, or some such, blondie?'

"Annie's a Professor of Organizational Behavior at Stanford," I said.

"My, my, is that so? And what's that then, when it's at home?"

"I study human communication," said Annie. "And I run seminars."

"Well, that's handy. Women fair like to blether."

"She's an educator, Dad, not a gossip." Annie clicked her tongue softly, a sign for me to shut up. I ignored her. "And anyway," I said. "I thought you didn't approve of women working."

"Doesn't sound very cheery." It was his turn to ignore me. "Dealing with students." He leaned forward and tapped Annie's knee with his pipe. "Guess most of them just need a swift kick up the arse, eh?"

"Pretty much," she laughed. "Yeah, pretty much."

I put another two fingers worth of whisky in my glass and stretched out in the armchair. The worn cover barely concealed the springs needling my back. Even in the faltering light, I could see yellow patches on the ceiling, moldy with damp and tobacco smoke.

Annie rose and chivvied Lauren to bed, then came back to collect Jacob. My father offered to carry him, but Annie said she would manage. A man who had never risen to help my mother with any heavy load, who never cocked his ear with interest as she jabbered on about her hopes, a man who instructed her to sell her piano because she was a poor player and he couldn't bear to hear her practice, and anyway it was too expensive to bring a tuner over from Oban every time dampness curdled its strings, this same man now offered to help my wife and child to bed.

"Would you like a glass of water?" he asked, when Annie returned, droopy with fatigue, to say goodnight to us both.

"No, thank you."

She ruffled the top of my hair, hesitated, then kissed my father on the cheek.

"Hold your horses, blondie," he said. "Hang on, now." He stood up, rather unsteadily, then dug around in first one pocket of his cardigan and then the other. He brought something out and placed it in her palm—a set of cameo earrings and a brooch.

"I don't understand..." she said. She glanced over at me then back at him.

"They belonged to Angus's mother."

"They're beautiful, I couldn't ..."

He folded her hand over them. "It's just a wee minder."

After she left, I placed my glass on the table. "I thought you'd given all Mum's stuff to Iona."

"See what thought did?"

"But Mum died yonks ago."

"I kept a few things back. For your Annie and your Lauren—but I was buggered if I was posting them. I knew you'd turn up given time."

I left him refilling his pipe and went outside to look at the stars. There were no stars. Low clouds smothered the peninsular. I tasted their thick dampness. I walked away from the cottage until its lights cast no relief on the heaviness around me and stopped when my stumbling was liable to lead to hurt. The sea breathed behind me while the soil sucked at my feet and swallowed the soles of my leather shoes. The nearest a man can come to death is to stand at night on our land. I'd forgotten how much I missed it in the constant brightness of America, where the day's end brings not true darkness but merely the temporary absence of light.

Dawn slipped under the window blind. I rolled over on the inflatable mattress and reached for Annie, but she wasn't there. I sat up, flustered, my heart thudding, my palm resting on the warm imprint where she'd lain.

The door opened. Annie tiptoed into the room, clutching a towel and her toiletries. She wore my sweater over her flannelette pajamas and shivered in the cold. The children still slept soundly on the single bed, their heads at opposite ends and their legs tangled in the center, our coats piled on top for extra warmth.

Annie sat on the edge of the mattress. I lay back down; I didn't want to meet her gaze. The cottage felt even more awful this morning than yesterday and I knew what she'd seen every time she'd visited the bathroom: old magazines piled up at the side of the tub, tobacco shreds bunched behind the cistern, taps crispy with rust, seagull shit on the broad window ledge. I waited for her to say something, words poised on my lips to defend him. After a moment of expectant silence, I glanced at her. She was tugging a large-toothed comb through her unruly curls, the faint mist of her breath visible in the chilled air.

"Sure doesn't feel like June," she whispered.

"It's early yet."

She rested the comb on her lap. "Did you talk to him last night?"

"About what?"

She shook her head and resumed tugging at her hair.

"You can't tell my father anything."

"Have you tried?"

I rolled over to face the wall.

"Angus, you promised Iona."

After quarreling with our father when she was fifteen, Iona had bought a one-way bus ticket from Kilchoan village to Glasgow. She found a job in a fish and chippie and moved in with a couple of other girls, then worked in a second-hand bookshop, then a college stationers, shifting to better positions and to better flats, till eventually administrating the largest library in the city. She gave me a bed the night I stopped by, fourteen years later, on my way to start my engineering degree in Edinburgh. The eleven year gap in our ages had turned us from siblings to strangers, a chasm we'd reduced inch by inch since then without bridging it completely. My father had made a deal with me; I could attend university provided I returned to help him on the croft after graduation. I didn't. An American company recruited me on the spot, and I left Scotland two weeks later, my mother's written blessing in my pocket, my father's anger at my back.

Annie's upbringing couldn't have been more different. She still called her parents every other day. Argued vociferously about everything. Yakked for hours about nothing. Ended every exchange with "I love you."

"When I'm with your father," she continued quietly, "I feel as if I'm drowning, but I don't care."

"He drives me up the wall." I twisted round to touch her face.

She rose, went to the window, and prized the stained plastic slats apart with her fingers. "Lord, it's breathtaking here," she said, softly. "What a pity we didn't visit sooner."

I sat up, bringing my knees to my chest. "When I was young," I said, "I used to sit at that window on school mornings and watch the trawlers come back from the night fishing. You could tell by the height and direction of the lights moving in the dark whose boat it was."

"Is there an airport?"

"Only three hours away."

"Only!" She laughed softly, then looked at me. She put her comb down. "You're serious, aren't you?"

I didn't reply. She gathered up her clothes, turning her back on me while she got dressed.

A few years ago when Annie had been expecting Jacob, we went to the launch of the new Wegmans grocery store outside Berkley. Annie always looked radiant when she was pregnant, still lithe and brown, but as though she'd stuffed a soccer ball up her shirt. We drifted along the aisles, sampling all the freebies, Lauren at our side clutching a balloon, her mouth stained pink from candy.

It was in the international foods section that my heart began to thump. An unbearable, nervous fluttering rose from my gut, followed by cresting wave after wave of nausea. I flushed hot then cold, and the floor began to ebb and heave beneath me, as though someone was flapping one end of it like a sheet.

"I think it must be sympathy pangs," I told Annie, squatting down and closing my eyes, because the symptoms matched her description of morning sickness. She stood over me, with her hand resting between my shoulder blades, while I waited for the feeling to pass. I felt like a right dip-stick—a grown man brought to his knees in a Californian grocery from the combined effect of *The Proclaimers* on the sound system and a display of Dundee thick-shred marmalade.

My father made porridge in the iron pot he'd used during my childhood. Jacob's bowl bulged with multicolored cereal shaped like alphabet letters.

"Mom," said Lauren, "This sugar will make him so hyper." She fiddled with a small collection of jewelry resting on her plate.

"I'm sure it won't do any harm, sweet pea." Annie dunked a teabag into a tin mug. "Just this once."

Jacob picked up the plastic catapult from the cereal box and propelled a letter across the kitchen. It bounced off the boiler and skittered under the fridge.

Lauren assumed an expression of smug satisfaction. Jacob looked at me swiftly, then at his grandfather and back. Considering the state of the kitchen, I felt it was pointless to warn about making a mess. Annie and I exchanged glances, negotiating which of us would issue the reprimand, but we waited too long. Jacob murmured an apology and the opportunity passed.

My father lifted the pot from the stove and poured its contents into a chipped brown dish. "You decided not to inflict your porridge on the kids, then," I said. The porridge burped like lava, the color and consistency of wet cement. "You always made me eat it."

"Aye, well." He dusted it liberally with salt. "Times change."

He sat down at the table and began to eat. He ate with his head bent, resting each mouthful on his tongue for the same amount of time, clutching a spoon in a shaky, liver-spotted fist. Everything around him, near him, on him, was peeling—a crofter's decay. Small flakes of scalp drifted from his thinning gray hair and rested on the threadbare elbows of his cardigan. The surface of the table, scored by years of dicing and chopping, had legs chewed by dogs long dead that tapered like blunt pencils to meet the crinkly linoleum coating the damp, stone floor. He was old. The house was old. I wanted him to forgive me for leaving.

My father tossed the spoon into the empty dish and sat up straight.

"So," he said. "It's the land you're after."

"We're not after anything," I said.

"It'll belong to you and Iona one day—and what'll happen then, eh? I know she can't wait to get rid of it and pocket the change."

"That's not fair, Iona needs the money to make a nice home for you ..."

"I told you, I'm no going."

"...and the land isn't the issue here. Your health is the

issue."

"Oh, it is, is it?

"She told me all about the rheumatism, and the chest pains."

"Your sister has a mouth the size of the Clyde tunnel."

"And the fall. Did you or did you not fall down in the pantry while bringing in peat and Iona had to drive up here four weekends in a row?"

"Would that have been the night of the fourteenth between the hours of eight and ten?"

Annie laughed, then apologized as my father glanced in her direction. Jacob looked distraught, wondering if he would be required to choose between his dad and his newly discovered and, no doubt, already favorite, grandparent. Tutting under her breath, Lauren crossed her skinny legs, picked up a ring and tried it on every finger. I realized, with a shock, that it was my mother's engagement ring.

"Be careful with that, Lauren, it's not a toy."

"I know!" She put it down on the plate and folded her arms. "Duh."

"You can't take it with you, Angus," my father said.

I frowned at him, baffled, before I understood what he meant. And he was wrong, for I could and I had. I carried it over the freeways of California; I carried it from exit to exit through a suburban grid crisscrossed by asphalt and plotted by fire hydrants—at every moment, of every day, of every week of my life, the wind and rain of my country tap, tap, tapped at my back, in an attempt to force me to turn around and remember.

I'd determined not to have a debate in front of the children about the impracticality of him remaining in this house. I kept my mouth shut about how I worried about him staying here, in this increasing isolation, and facing those winter storms, birthed full-formed off the coast of the New World, that crossed the Atlantic and arrived, furious as harpies, to batter at his door. Realizing his attempt to skirmish had failed, my father slid his gaze over to Jacob.

"So, do you still want to be a spaceman?"

"No," said Jacob, "A crofter."

"Good lad."

I took my mug to the sink and looked out the open window. The country beguiled with a gloriously sunny morning. The islands of Rum, Eigg, and Muck sat in a placid sea, perfectly delineated as if by a purple crayon. A light breeze ruffled the long grasses rimming the cliff and puffed the scents of honeysuckle and seaweed onto my face.

My father and Jacob took alternate shots of the catapult to try and hit me from behind with pieces of cereal. As each piece fell, I lifted it up and placed it on the draining board. So it's true, I thought, scooping the pile of letters into the bin, grandchildren provide the opportunity to atone for what one has done to one's own children.

Annie took the cereal box from Jacob and sealed its lid. She placed it in the pantry and came to stand beside me at the window. My father joined us.

"Wouldn't you like to see this always, blondie?" He nudged her with his shoulder. "I'll bet no many folk back in your America own a view like that, eh?"

Annie fixed her gaze on the horizon. She waited for me to respond on our behalf, but I, too, wanted to hear what she would say. Both my father and I paused, alert for her verdict, but she kept her counsel.

"Do you fancy a stretch of the legs?" he said, at last. I glanced at Annie.

"You two go." She turned her back on my silent plea for help. "We're going to have a toast and marmalade party."

The leather shoes I'd worn the night before sat on the mat, encrusted with mud. Determined to make no special purchases for our visit, I'd brought only one pair. My father pulled on his unlaced boots and took another pair from a wooden crate by the sink.

"Here," he said. "Wear these, and leave those ponsy things to decompose."

He stood up and was out the door before I'd even adjusted my socks. Annie shooed the kids from the kitchen, then collected the jewelry from Lauren's plate.

"I'll send these to Iona," she said.

"I thought you liked the jewelry."

"I do," Annie said. "It's exquisite."

"So, where's the harm ..."

"Can't you see what he's doing?"

"What?"

"You've got to convince him to sell it, not just for Iona's sake but for ours."

"Look, there's an easier solution, Annie, I didn't want to say but ..."

"I know what you're going to ask, but no. I can't risk it. Just owning it wouldn't be enough for you."

My father's head popped up abruptly at the kitchen window. He tapped the glass. "Is it today you're coming, son, or tomorrow?" he shouted, then disappeared.

When I turned back, Annie had gone. The door slammed behind her. I wrestled, pissed off, with both the knots in the grotty laces of his old boots and with Annie's parting shot, before I managed to untangle one and get the boots on, and shunt the other into a dark cellar in my mind and slam yet another door.

My father had already crossed the path by the cliffs, his stride confident, as I scuttled along, trying to keep up. As I gained on him, his swaggering gait became forced and unsteady, so I hung back, keeping the distance between us the same as it always had been. We stopped to watch the waves skirling at the foot of the cliffs. I toyed with the nettles at my feet with the toes of his boots.

"We'd be abandoning her, you know." He nodded toward a grave overlooking the ocean and marked by a Celtic stone cross. "She was a good woman, your mother."

"I'm sure she'd have liked to have heard you say that."

"How the hell would you know what your mother and I said to each other when she was alive?" I took a step back. "Or what I say to her now she's gone, come to think of it."

He took the path down to the beach. I paused for a moment before trailing after him.

"And I don't remember you rushing much to your mother's defense," he tossed over his shoulder. "Though you hid behind her skirts often enough." He swirled around. "This isn't California you know, Angus. We don't go around dropping 'love' into everything like dandruff. Just because we hold our peace doesn't mean we've nothing to say."

"You've plenty to say this trip."

"I reckon so have you or you wouldn't have dragged yourselves and those bairns all the way over here, though you've yet to spit whatever it is out."

He headed onto the beach. I looked back up to the cottage. During my childhood, my mother hung out washing on this hill. I'd carry the basket of clothes pegs, to stop it being kicked around by the blustery weather. She'd select two pegs and hold them in her mouth while she wrestled a sheet onto the line, securing a corner with one peg, then the other. Finally, more often than not, she raised a hand to shield her eyes and stared across the sea.

"Over there is America, Angus," she'd say. I'd follow her gaze to the empty horizon. "That's where your uncles are."

Her tone was wistful, yet defiant. I didn't want to cross that ocean. Our hill wasn't high enough to see what was on the other side. We would leave the sheets waving like large white flags toward the west, proof of our existence—or perhaps of our capitulation.

My father stood where the brown arc of seaweed bordered the shore. I swithered between joining him or returning to Annie and the kids, but I couldn't suppress the memories of my mother. I stumbled across the beach until we met face to face.

"The piano," I said. "Is that something you discuss with her now she's gone?"

"What are you on about?" He tucked his pipe between his teeth.

"You know fine well. Mum's piano."

"What piano?" He reached into another pocket and took out a tobacco pouch. "Your mother never had a piano."

"Yes, she did." I crossed my arms. "And you made her sell it."

"How could I have made her sell it, if she didn't have it, you daft eejit?"

My father, his face creased with concentration, returned the tobacco pouch to his pocket. Then: "Ach, that'd be old Mrs. McFadden from the croft further around the bay you're thinking of. They brought it along the shoreline and up our hill." He started to laugh, pressing the wad of tobacco flat with a thick thumb. "Your mother was that livid with Jack MacFadden, she never stopped talking about it for years."

He pulled out a box of matches and struck one, cupping his hand to protect its feeble flare. Catching my eyes, his laughter trailed off.

"Christ sakes, Angus," he said, and threw the match into the sea. "All that California sunshine's addled your brain." He pursed his lips and began to walk. "It's about time you got yourself away from the land of fruit and nuts, my boy."

The sand shifted beneath my feet. I took a step back from the incoming tide, and saw my footprints dissolve and disappear.

By the week's end I knew my misgivings about returning here had been justified. Like a patriotic lush, I was buckling under the dangerous seductiveness of my home country, captivated by the scent of peat, by the polished gray stone of the uneven pantry floor, by the weather that lifted and fell like sheets as the day tossed and turned into night. Our visit opened up the false possibility of choice, exactly the outcome I'd determined to prevent. We belonged in California, as Annie had implied. I refused to revisit that decision again. To leave home once is enough.

My father, pleased with his handiwork (to him, his attributes and those of Scotland were indistinguishable), began to reel my wife and children in with tales about the country, tales he'd omitted to share with me when I was child. Or perhaps he had, and I couldn't remember them. I said nothing, entranced by his art and appalled by his brazenness. How had he suddenly become so talkative? This man, who, in my youth, believed the niceties of politeness were wasted on family and should be kept, like the willow pattern wedding china, for Sundays and visitors? In retrospect, I understood that his volubility illustrated his desperation to save what little he could, to gain a little time, to secure a little ground.

I envied his assurance, his lack of doubt, and his six feet in height, for I carried my mother's build and my mother's temerity, and I watched in despair as my smart wife allowed him to question the worth of her opinions — exactly as he had with me years before. Annie's eyes sparkled with good-humor over his bullying banter about modern women, and modern ways, and modern children, and modern ideals. My wife's swift acceptance of the virtues of "over here" against the vices of "over there" (proof of her attempt to be agreeable), gave him the impression that she might be convinced. There were so many reasons why we couldn't leave America that her mock capitulation was the cruelest thing she could have done.

She let him cut her down with the swift, swishing efficiency of a sickle through dry wheat. Only my daughter still held ground like a tenacious, wiry stalk. Not due to the wit of her arguments, no, but by a simple, adolescent determination not to open her small, grim mouth.

As the minutes ticked into hours, his desperate onslaught dwindled and first Jacob, then Lauren, and finally my wife, fell asleep, exhausted by so much fresh air and cunning, their heads tilted toward him like dependent eaves propping up his particular view of the world.

Before bed I called Iona, and told her that I'd failed.

"That's us." Annie closed the boot of the car. Lauren and Jacob had already said their goodbyes and sat in the back arguing over the portable DVD. Down on the beach, I could see him wandering along the shoreline.

"I'll wait here." Annie slipped into the passenger seat. She closed the door and picked up the map. After a few minutes she wound the window down. "It's highly unlikely that your father's personality is going to change at this point in his life so I suggest you get on with it," she said, then wound the window back up.

With a gesture of sympathy for my ruined shoes, my father moved back beyond the seaweed and met me well above the crest of the tide. We watched the waves from the safety of the rocks.

"Dad," I said. "Have you nothing to say about the piano?"

He sifted a handful of sand through blackened fingers. "Don't pretend to know the secrets of other folks' marriages," he said. "Lord knows I can't begin to understand the mystery of yours." He handed me a shell. "I've no idea what that lassie saw in you."

I rolled the shell around in my palm. As my father watched the sea, his normal expression slipped away. The guarded cockiness dissolved into the frail tremulousness of an old man, an old man with eyes brimming with fear, fear that his son would desert this landscape that he loved with such ferociousness, it defied common sense. He had been taught that to love something one must always be present. How could his son be part of this peninsula, or this beach, or this particular ribbon of kelp if he were absent? How can love exist when the lover is missing?

"Listen," he said, bending so close I smelled the ashy tang of mothballs and tobacco on his clothes. "Help your sister out."

"I would if I could, but I'm nowhere near as comfortable financially as you think. And it's my fault you think I am. I was showing off."

"But what about her." He jerked his head toward the car, where Annie sat waiting. "Her business is ticking along champion, she told me."

"That's not going to happen."

"She's your wife, isn't she?"

"It's complicated... Anyway none of this solves the problem of you living here on your own."

"Let's you and me do a wee deal."

"We're not doing any deals, Dad."

"Oh, is it the idea of a deal that worries you? You're no so good at those, are you? You did a runner on our last one."

I turned away.

"Aw, dry your eyes, son." He caught my sleeve and shuffled closer. "Listen," he whispered, as though we were surrounded by eavesdroppers. "I've made up my mind. I'll go to Glasgow and live with Iona and that daft husband of hers—though God knows he's a spare part—and I'll even fork out for her bloody house renovations—if, and only if, she forfeits her half of the land after I'm gone."

"Iona doesn't give two hoots about the land, Dad."

"I know, son, but you do."

Brushing the sand from his hands, he walked back to the cottage, abandoning me at the shoreline, moored to that melancholy country—that country that exists between where I was born and where I am now, neither here nor there, neither one thing nor another.

# The Housekeeper

I KNEW AS SOON AS I SAW HER, this situation was going to take some work. She were skinny and pale—real ladies are always akin to greyhounds—a tad leggy, a tad skittery. Eyebrows plucked near gone. Her hair, skin, and frock all the one color like lard.

I stood in the morning room while she read my references, a chandelier above me—Irish, I'd say—Lord knows the last time those crystals saw water. She smoked a cigarette, curled up on the chaise longue. I know it's the fashion but I've never liked to see a lady smoke and moreover the ashtray hadn't been emptied since the last one. Told a tale about the current state of affairs and no mistake.

"You come very highly recommended, Mrs. Braithwaite," she said. Braithwaite's my married name, but I'm a widow now, and my employers seem to prefer it that way. No worries about hanky panky on the back stairs—though I've never met a man I could stomach for more than five minutes. My Harold excepted, of course.

"Thank you, Ma'am," I said.

A very respectable household by all accounts, I'd heard, for I'm picky with my situations. Two children, mind you, but between the nursery, the garden, and homework I'd be able to keep them from under my feet. And there would be no butler to contend with neither. The war had drafted them all away to fight the Hun. With any luck they'd die for their country and give those of us who know what we're about a bit of peace.

"Yes," she finished in that whispery voice of hers. "I think you'll do nicely." I decided right there and then that I'd get her maid up a half-hour earlier to heat irons for her hair. It looked right wispy and limp.

But sloppy hairdressing were just the tip of the iceberg—rugs not beaten for months, brass doorknobs and fenders dull as dishwater, enough fluff under beds to knit pullovers for a whole battalion, and whoever had been in charge before thought tape on the windows meant they'd never need cleaned. I had the whole chore rota worked out in my head by the time the chauffeur came back from Kings Cross with my bags.

Once I had the housekeeper's parlor to my liking and put my Bible by the bed, I rolled up my sleeves and got right to it. I put more backbone in that staff in the first ten minutes than the previous housekeeper could've managed in a month of Sundays. Laundry bleached and pressed regular, fire grates blackened, chandeliers down and washed with boiling water and vinegar. In two weeks I'd everything whipped into shape but the floors, and those were the worst. Never seen a drop of beeswax.

I spent most of my time cleaning up after the Mistress— she were right jittery. I'd follow her around with a brush and a dustpan to scoop up shattered perfume bottles and wine glasses. At first I blamed the Blitz, but I soon realized it were him. He were a big man, the Master, with fat, fleshy, butcher hands. He'd worked hard to get rid of the Yorkshire in his voice, but he didn't fool me. I doubt he were more than two parishes shy of my own. Common.

Once she nearly missed the Ladies War Effort Committee luncheon at Claridges. Would have been well nigh a scandal, because the Mistress were Chairwoman. Elsie, the chambermaid, came looking for me. I were in the kitchen showing Tommy how to iron a newspaper proper without singeing the headlines.

"Oh, Mrs. Braithwaite," Elsie starts, all out of breath, "the Mistress…"

"Have you been running again?" There's nothing worse than a maid clattering up and down stairs. Especially our Elsie—built like an ocean liner only not quite so seaworthy. I left Tommy with the warning that I'd be buying no more extra copies of the *Times* starting tomorrow and he'd better practice on the brown paper that'd come wrapped round the fish.

The Mistress lay on her bed, shivering. I could hear the Master stomping around his room next door. The sheets were ruffled and stained after we'd spent the morning ironing both sides. I knew the Master's type. A tad like my Harold, bless him, he couldn't go about his business without making a mess neither. The Mistress's silk negligee stuck to her back with blood; the feathers from its collar and cuffs floating all over as though someone had just plucked a turquoise goose.

"Come along, Ma'm," I said. "Let's get you up." The Mistress vomited a dribble onto her lap. I reckon she'd bitten her tongue.

"Oh, Lord above, Mrs. Braithwaite," Elsie said, her jaw swinging like a gate. "We should get a doctor." A doctor indeed. A nosy parker with a stethoscope, more like.

"You shut your mouth, girl," I said. "You look like a railway tunnel." Thank God, our Elsie wasn't driving an ambulance. There'd be more casualties outside it than in.

"Run your Mistress's bath," I said. "Not too hot, mind— and get some Epsom salts from the kitchen." Elsie wound her apron round her hands and wiped it under her nose. "Now," I said, "and *walk* back."

I tweezed the feathers off the weals forming on the Mistress's shoulders before wrapping her in bandages we'd made from old sheets in case we were bombed out. After I gave her a brandy, she were right as rain.

"But I can't possibly go, Mrs. Braithwaite," she said.

"Nonsense, Ma'am," I said. "The ladies are relying on you." I took her new costume from the wardrobe. She'd had it made special; a navy blue suit with a peplum, white lace blouse, red shoes, and gloves. Very appropriate.

"This a time for us to be thinking about others, Ma'am," I said, removing tissue from the crown of her hat. "Not ourselves."

The Master were a right snappy dresser—paisley cravats, pin stripe suits, fedoras and Brylcreem. Good looking if you fancied a spiv. Dodged the draft because he worked for the government. One afternoon a trollop turned up and asked to see him. I soon sent her packing, once I'd managed to shift her rump from the front door to the back. She wore real silk stockings.

The Mistress had started to look more and more like a poor man's rack of lamb. She'd chase the food about her plate but barely eat a bite. The last thing I needed were her starving to death and it reported in the papers. I've never worked in a scandalous house before and I'd no intention of doing so now. Cook were always complaining about the number of eggs going to waste, but it wouldn't look proper if the sideboard weren't spread with a decent English breakfast. You keep scrambling an half-dozen, I told her, till I tell you otherwise. I've never had problems getting my mitts on eggs—nought's hard if you know what you're about, but polish were another kettle of fish entirely.

It took over three months to collect enough rations to cover the floors upstairs and down. Daisy gave them a right solid buffing and I helped out with the top landing. Wood came up champion. Only it weren't very slippery. I reckoned I needed that foreign muck. Hard to come by though, so I'd a quiet word with Jones, the coalman, who specialized in supplying articles of a very particular nature.

But the Mistress's children were a trial. They'd pester the living daylights out of her then run wild as heathens through my nice clean house. When Elsie set their tea out in the nursery, I'd turn the key on them. I liked to know where they were. They looked like a couple of poppets when their hair were brushed but they were a mess of questions and snippy looks and smart-alec answers, especially that boy.

Every time I got down on my knees at the top of the stairs to apply a bit of elbow grease, I'd find him watching me, looking like butter wouldn't melt in his mouth. I told the Mistress it would do no harm to take a slipper to him now and again but she wouldn't have it. Finally I convinced her that London were no place for children and they got packed off with other evacuees to a farm in Wales.

The Red Cross dinner party finished it. Cook had saved all the meat, butter, and sugar rations to put out a decent spread. We had to put two sets of blackout drapes on the dining room windows—there were that many candles.

Half-past seven and no sign of the Mistress in the drawing room and the Master's tugging at his collar. He sent me upstairs to fetch her. She's sat at her dressing table, hair all matted, in those green silk pajamas she wears for lounging about the house— the top half slipped off, her back pitted with bruises like a banana gone bad. Been years since I'd had a banana, I remember thinking.

"Now, M'am," I said, "we must pull ourselves together." I wrapped her limp arms around my neck, and dragged her into the bathroom. "We can't have them missing their charming hostess."

I helped her dress. She never said a word, just whimpered now and then like a dog. I told her to keep her chin up, the Master were relying on her. I chose a nice apricot satin gown with an high back and long sleeves that covered all his goings-on. Though he weren't daft. Like my Harold, he never hit where it showed. The frock were a bit low cut for my taste, but elegant nevertheless and no chance of her falling out and making a fool of herself—flat as a washboard.

Elsie helped with her hair. She kept asking the Mistress if she were all right. "Shut up, girl," I said to her. "You concentrate on those pins." We clipped diamante bits and bobs on the Mistress's ears, wrists, and bosom, then chivvied her down the stairs.

What a lovely meal—cream of mushroom soup, shrimps au gratin, spotted dick, real coffee with demerara lumps— you'd never have known there were a war on. Mentioned in the society pages the next day. *"It is a comfort to us all,"* it read, *"that the true virtues of the British character—charity, hospitality, courage and impeccable good taste are still to be found in abundance amongst society's brightest lights."*

Obviously after all that folderol, time had run out for the coalman. I'd have to use butter. Trouble was, Cook watched over the butter like it were gold bullion. It took me a couple of weeks to collect enough, stealing slivers from the pat with a cheese wire.

The Master must have been a cat in another life; he were right dainty on his pins. The first couple of tries, he hardly slithered an inch, just swore in that coarse way of his and kept going. Eventually, I took Cook's keys to the pantry, as it would need a right good dollop to set him off. Cook were livid. We had a scene that did neither of us any credit but I stuck to my guns.

The following morning, I got up before five and got the staff to their chores. Then I waited outside the Master's bedroom. His alarm clock had been set an half hour later. I heard him rushing in and out the adjoining door to the Mistress's room. "Bitch," he were saying. Finally he cleared his throat, as he always did after tying his shoelaces before heading down for breakfast. I rolled the rug away, leaving a pale streak of butter from his bedroom to the top of the stairs.

I waited till I heard his neck snap against the bottom step, then I drew a damp cloth over the floor, put the rug back and nipped down to wipe off the soles of his shoes.

The Mistress wailed like an air raid siren for weeks afterwards. I were right disappointed, I thought she'd be pleased, widowhood being so tidy like. And he'd been no great catch—a puffed up Yorkshire pudding with a terrible taste in neckties and no understanding of the way things are done.

Had to let Cook go too—a pity—but she never stopped tittle-tattling about pilfering. All the fuss is behind us now, though. The house is looking exactly as it should— you could eat your dinner off the floor. The new Cook were a bit of a trial with her fancy ideas about how to boil a brisket, but I soon saw to that.

# Letting George Down

THE MOST REMARKABLE EVENT of George's life happened after his death. He became known as "the fan who fell from the sky" and a small cult was born. A box was dedicated to him at the Molson Center and a plaque installed near the dimple he dented on Rue Saint Francois Xavier.

George's renown hinged, not on the value of his life, but on the manner of his leaving it. Louisa couldn't bear this yet bore it anyway. She collected fragments of her shattered heart from the ironing board, from the windowsill, from around his body on a pavement moist with spring. She needed them to survive letting George down.

Two players tussled for the puck. They slammed into the boards and one slid to the ice. His helmet fell off revealing a bloody nose and toothless gums mouthing obscenities while the other player swept the puck away. The television image sizzled around the edges.

George leaned forward. He radiated an odor like warm hops from too many days in his red plaid pajamas, the flannelette shrunken from too many laps in the tumble dryer, every second button missing. Hair plastered his forehead, his chin bristled with neglect, and his bony feet dangled from the footrest of the purple leather recliner in jacquard socks and rabbit fur slippers.

He stabbed at the remote control. White lines bolted across the television like a heartbeat monitor. He tensed his calves until the leg-rest twanged home, then dragged his recliner across the carpet using his heels.

Snow on the screen mimicked the view out the window. Winter had kidnapped Montréal and gagged it with powder and ice. George stood up and thumped the television with a sweaty fist. A vase of plastic irises fell off and bounced on the shag rug. He'd told Louisa to get cable but she never listened to him. Admittedly, George rarely spoke these days except to swear. In two languages.

"Mon oiste d'tabernak, he said. "You fucking piece of shit."

George stepped outside his triangular comfort zone of television, recliner and beer. The rash courageousness of this act only struck him once it had passed, and now he felt capable of anything. He slipped the remote control into the breast pocket of his pajamas—over his heart—then pulled a sweatshirt with Canadiens printed across its chest from the laundry pile. He kept his slippers on and added a balaclava and mittens. Looking like a cozy bank robber, George left the apartment for the first time in two months.

The former Canadian Pacific Telegraph building towered over old Montréal with the curlicue presumptuousness of the nineteenth century. Tenants never visited its roof between October and May because of the weather. George hoisted the iron bar that blocked the door, the metal caterwauling in protest, and tried to push it open. He slammed his shoulder against it until he felt the snow bank splinter, and then he squeezed through the resulting gap.

The roof was as smooth and treacherous as a hockey rink. George slithered almost all the way to its precipitous edge before he managed to stop. He tottered, breathless, knees bent, above the smoldering city. Steam billowed from chimneys and vents, potholes and car exhausts, subway stations and horse manure. The river, not yet completely frozen, coiled away from the harbor to the east, a black snake between two carpets of lights.

The aluminum television aerial stood three feet in from the roof edge and rose twenty feet high. George looked up at the receiver bar that bisected its trunk like a cross. He stretched toward it but couldn't reach. Up there, somewhere, in a sky dizzy with snowflakes, was his problem.

After a smidgen of deliberation, George wrapped his arms around the trunk and began to haul himself upward. It was hard going because he was out of shape and sweat began to trickle from his pores, but mania driven by desperation overcame months of sloth and propelled him on. When he looked up again, he was almost close enough to fiddle with the cross bar.

Holding on with knotted legs and one arm, he stretched out the other, the aerial already muttering like a metallic Cassandra about its ability to support his weight. His brain registered the noise, along with a nebulous realization of the precariousness, not to mention the ludicrousness, of his situation, not unlike the distant whistle of a faraway train that inspires a fleeting alarm but precipitates little immediate action. His senses were suffocated, his ears blocked by damp wool, his nose and mouth sealed by an intricate lace of ice embroidered by his erratic breath. Tiny pyramids, crusty as sea salt, rimmed his eyes, and his fingers, trapped in the clump of the mittens, couldn't feel what they were doing. Using his teeth, he pulled the first mitten off and let it go. Then turned to bite off the other.

As the second mitten fell, the trunk of the aerial emitted a low moan, bent under his weight and swung out over the edge of the building. George plummeted forward, head first, toward its tip. Stars, lights and smoke appeared to whoosh past him, and then judder to a halt. He coiled his body around the trunk in a frantic embrace causing his pajamas to scrunch into lumps at his thighs and under his armpits, uncovering skin slippery with sweat. After the aerial stopped vibrating, George, gingerly, tried to push himself backwards along its length to the roof of the building and safety, but his movements caused it to lurch even lower and exposed more of his flesh to the night air.

George lay still, his arms gripping the cross bar. The full train of thought regarding his predicament careened around the last bend of comprehension and screeched to a halt, steaming, in the center of his brain.

Winter plucked the tiny stitches of moisture from his skin and knitted them to the aluminum as he clung, inert, helpless, ten floors above Rue Saint Francois Xavier.

Louisa tucked containers of pasta amatriciana under her chin and dug in her bag for her keys. She'd visited her mother on her way home to pick up some food and moan about George. He didn't look at her anymore and she wasn't used to being ignored. As she put her key in the lock, she noticed the door stood ajar.

"George?" she said.

Louisa dumped the food on the kitchen counter, removed her rubber boots and went into the living room. George wasn't there. She focused hard to make sure. Empty rooms often felt emptier when George was in them. The television was on, broadcasting an uncharacteristically crisp image of the game between the Montréal Canadiens and the Ottawa Senators. The Canadiens were winning four-nil.

The recliner and beer looked bereft, like the much-mauled debris from a yard sale. Louisa felt a flicker of annoyance. The room was a tip. He might tidy up once in a while. She lifted the vase of plastic irises off the shag rug and put it back on top of the television then turned to the table to peel an open packet of cooked ham off a sports magazine.

She changed into leggings and a t-shirt before plastering her face with expensive mud and climbing onto a pink exercise bike. She might as well do twenty minutes while waiting for George to turn up.

Louisa was not heartless or immune to flights of fancy, but she lacked emotional intuitiveness. While others might have found the unlocked apartment, the unfinished beer, the sports announcer in the loud suit lobbing his opinions toward the empty recliner, somewhat alarming, Louisa found the lack of George too absurd to merit serious consideration. The possibility that he may have grown tired of her buxom charms or fallen ill never crossed her mind.

Wow, she thought, pedaling hard, watching the ice hockey, my eyesight is improving — I can actually see the puck.

If Louisa could have pedaled out of the apartment and up the stout exterior wall of the former Canadian Pacific Telegraph building to its slithery roof, she would have seen the island of Montréal clogging the artery of the St. Lawrence river, she would have seen the twinkling pulses of a million dormant lives, and she would have seen what was visible only from the impassive black heaven above, a man bonded to the cross of an aerial.

George heard the roof door slip shut. In a while, a fresh blanket of ice would tuck it snug as an army cot till spring. It had stopped snowing. At first, his muscles had ached with the strain of holding on until he realized that his fusion with the aerial was so complete that he could relax and not fall off. Shouting for help was hopeless — breathing was agony, speech impossible. Down below, the few passersby were buckled over with cold and mortality. Some, if not most, had spent lifetimes without looking up.

The spires of Notre Dame Cathedral scraped at the stars. Beyond gleamed the steely Molson Center, the new home of the Canadiens. He had never been to see a match; he'd not be able to bear it — too many people combined with the terror of live action. After all, they might lose.

He turned his head to the river. If he could follow its

black course over the horizon he would eventually reach his hometown of Trois-Rivières. His English-Canadian parents still lived there, in complacent and mutual detestation, besieged by the French. Inside the small clapboard house he had been George, outside, Georges.

Indecisiveness had muddled his early years. His parents shilly-shallied over language choice, vegetarianism, and methods of child-raising—disciplinarian versus loosey-goosey. They chose not to decide rather than risk a wrong decision. His mother had cared for nothing but George's future occupation. She lost interest in who he was when she realized that what he would do would probably be of little import to the world at large. Eventually, his father forgot about him completely, once or twice tripping over toys in the hall, bending down to pick them up, perplexed. George had grown up bilingual and ignored. He spent his time hiding up trees or under tables. Anywhere—as long as he was out of the way.

Louisa stuck a container of pasta in the microwave and waited for the ping.

Since George had lost his job, Louisa felt he'd been shrinking. He had worked for Dodgy Jacques, the owner of a window-glazing firm locked in a turf battle with rivals on both sides of the Québec-Ontario border. George had toiled on the sly, like many of Jacques's employees, being paid in cash while picking up his unemployment check. After he refused to take part in a questionable contract involving patio doors, a Masonic lodge and a former member of the Bloc Québécois, Jacques had fired him.

Over the next three years, his job applications reduced to a trickle. He seemed to become smaller and wizened, skulking around the apartment like a damp cat, saying little yet well-behaved, a slight abrasion in Louisa's domestic bliss, like dropped socks, crumbs in the bed, hairs in the sink.

She looked at the television. George had inched closer to it in the past few days. Maybe it had swallowed him? She visualized his final moments as the soles of his slippers had been sucked, whirling, through the screen, accompanied by an enormous, satisfied slurp like an airplane toilet. She peeked around the back. He wasn't there.

Louisa considered hunting for George in all the small places in the apartment. Perhaps she should look in the kitchen cupboards and the refrigerator, open cereal packets, cookie jars and cartons of ice cream. Shake pasta boxes by her ear like tambourines and lift empty beer bottles to her eye like telescopes. Root around in the cutlery drawer, the vegetable bin and the tea caddy where they kept loose change. Take the lids off painkillers, toothpaste, pots and pans. Unzip her make-up bag, gym bag, and finally her purse, dangle it upside down by her fingertips until keys, lipsticks, parched chewing gum balled in tissue, vitamins, metro tickets and dusty jelly beans spilled onto the kitchen table where they would skitter to all four corners in a cloud of barely beige face powder.

But that would be irrational. People don't shrink and disappear. The microwave pinged behind her.

"George?" she said.

Since George had lost his job, he felt he'd been shrinking. The underground economy had been neither lucrative nor safe. Battles between the window-glazing companies often resulted in front-line casualties and one or two of his buddies succumbed every winter. The lucky ones surfaced in spring, suddenly bobbing bloated on the river like buoys or sieved from mounds of snow beside the former path of a plough. The unlucky completely disappeared.

But you can get used to anything. In summer, he mourned; in winter, he lived. He lived for days when it was so cold that his eyelashes stuck together and he'd have to peel them apart to count the dollars from his wallet at the beer store, before going home to watch the game.

Without his job, he had nothing but the winter. He discovered that the jobless slip through the cracks of the living. He dreaded simple questions. What do you do? How was your day? My day was the same as every other day. I do nothing. His friends evaporated along with his funds and he sank into the nameless mass of the unemployed, people with quiet wants and average ability, propelled to and fro by history and economics like marbles on a manhole cover. George became the pause between sentences, never the subject of them.

Louisa had taken over his apartment and his life. She was exhausting, exuberant, intoxicating: the red wine, the pasta, the tantrums, the plastic flowers, the curling irons and face creams crowding the small shelf in the bathroom. She had commandeered his side of the wardrobe, blunted his razors on her fleshy legs, force fed him risotto and insisted he floss. She marched him to date movies and demanded popcorn and participation. She pestered him to articulate his feelings and became defensive and weepy when they differed from her own. Every now and then she would leap on top of him in the middle of the night, rip the buttons off his pajamas and churn like a washing machine.

When George's buddies met Louisa, they soon forgot about George. Louisa was proof that men didn't care about weight. She had wanted to start a family because she felt she was getting old. She was twenty-three.

"We could have babies," she said. "They'd pay us to bring them up speaking French—they do that, you know."

"But you don't speak French." George couldn't risk children. They'd all be girls. They'd all look like her. He would be enveloped, surrounded, corralled.

"I can learn," she persisted. "I could." Soon, he thought, Louisa would swallow him completely and there would be nothing left of him but a burp.

Louisa flicked open her diary and searched the entries looking for clues about George. After scanning her purple, loopy text, she realized that he was rarely mentioned. She shut the diary, turned out the light, and scrunched down under the comforter.

Was George happy? Why wouldn't he be? She did her best. She fed him, cleansed him and loved him. She had found him so easy to live with, so quiet and undemanding, like a goldfish. She wanted to marry him and start a family although George was reluctant. She couldn't think of a greater gift than a child, to give him back a part of himself and, not coincidently, give him something to do.

He didn't need much sex either—a great relief as Louisa considered lovemaking within the realm of the domestic chore, and applied to it the same resigned but ruthless vigor she applied to scouring the kitchen sink. Nevertheless, she didn't skimp her favors because her mother, Mama Baldetti, had told her that intimate relations were important to masculine health and well-being. So Louisa did her best to flush George out twice a week, Wednesdays and Saturdays. Sometimes, he hadn't even awoken. Denied, men became blocked, her mother told her, like drains.

The ice on George's eyelashes reduced his vision to a letterbox slit. A horse and carriage clattered beneath him. Hired no doubt, he thought, by a tourist who had planned it as a prelude to seduction but whose balls were now in the process of freezing prior to falling off.

George imagined walking down Rue Saint Francois Xavier, then right onto Rue Saint Paul and following it till it ended at Rue Berri before turning back for home. He had marched these streets looking for work, but as his crusade faltered he avoided public places for everyone he met was embarrassed by his failure. George noticed that people greeted each other differently depending on what they did. Eyes gladdened at the doctor, glazed over the plumber and closed at the unemployed.

To avoid pity or condemnation, he had stripped his conversation down to hockey and bilingual expletives.

George could no longer feel his fingers and toes, those same digits where he'd experienced that strange shrinking sensation after he'd lost his job, that curling, burning itch. More like decomposing, actually, say leaves shriveling at the edges, brittle and destined for dust. He had begun to avoid daylight, pressing himself close to walls fearful lest he no longer cast a shadow and wishing to save his former friends the awkwardness of denying him. Night walks ended too. Too dangerous to his contracting, crusty frame. One misstep could plunge him down a storm drain or freeze his extremities till they snapped like hard candy. Such probabilities did not strike him as strange. He read in the newspapers about the fish that walked on land, the hole in the roof of the world, and the dead brought back to life by the transplanted organs of others.

The fairy lights on the Molson Center winked at him. His breath was so faint it no longer chalked the air. He didn't care. The pain was gone. He had met his mis-step and it wasn't so bad. Winter conquered his body. Everything numbed. He felt a strange contentment, a lulling of despondency. The blood that had failed to save his limbs rushed back through his veins and surged into his chest with a burst of warmth and a sensation not so different from joy.

George closed his eyes; he felt nothing but his heart.

The following morning Louisa called Dodgy Jacques, in case a job had turned up. Jacques denied any knowledge of George's whereabouts, though that meant little, he never openly acknowledged his employees, or his creditors, or any of his offspring scattered around Montréal like bird droppings. He told Louisa she was a gorgeous girl. He told her George had no business living with her outside of wedlock. He told her of his last conversation with George, when George had refused to transact that little bit of business for him in Ottawa.

"And so, ma belle Lou-Lou," said Jacques, "you can see how it was."

"Well, not really, no."

"You think I was unreasonable?"

"Well, actually, yes."

Jacques apologized and asked Louisa out to dinner. Louisa refused. She told him that she'd like to but she'd lost something and planned to remove her faucets and check the pipes. She imagined Jacques's fat hand slithering down the front of his elasticized pants as soon as she hung up the phone.

Louisa decided to return to her family until George turned up. The Baldettis lived in Plateau Mont Royal in a double duplex. Mama, Papa, Grandma and Grandpa lived on one side and Aunt Sophia and Uncle Tony on the other. Aunt Sophia spent all day making pasta and the family spent all evening eating it. Three times a week, before George stopped going out at all, Louisa and George had dined with her family on the Plateau. The Baldettis did their best to make George feel at home by laying out their lumpy welcome mat of tough love.

"You're not eating enough," Aunt Sophia would say.

"You don't get out enough," Mama Baldetti would say.

"You should get a decent job," Uncle Tony would say.

"So, you gonna marry my princess, or what?" Papa Baldetti would say.

"You never say anything," Louisa would say, as they plodded home together through the slush.

Two weeks after George's disappearance, Louisa contacted the police. George's lack of distinguishing features failed to tickle the interviewing officer's interest. The woman asked Louisa what kind of man he was.

"Nice," Louisa said.

"Irrelevant," the officer replied. She wanted facts. First, what did he do for a living and, second, did he engage in criminal activity, frequent brothels, dodge taxes, drink too much, beat Louisa up? Third, was he liable to commit suicide or go nuts?

"Oh, no," Louisa said, when the officer had finished her recitation of human frailties, "he would never do anything like that."

During the first flush of their romance, Louisa had flooded into George's apartment. Her belongings seeped into every available nook and cranny and began a systematic erosion of anything that belonged to George. Against the rising tide of her trappings and affection, George had attempted to sandbag territory with wardrobe partitions and double towel hooks, sticky nametags and 'his and her' junk drawers. Following the collapse of his job search, he submitted gracefully to a final submersion by giving everything away that anyone else might want in the hope that people, including Louisa, would leave him alone. The result was a tiny island of stuff on the second shelf in the hall cupboard.

Louisa laid out the detritus of George's life on the kitchen table: several pairs of faded pajamas (buttons missing), nail clippers, a glaziers tool kit, copies of the NHL schedules for the current and previous seasons, a collection of microbrewery beer mats, and a signed photograph of Mario Tremblay.

How could she know if anything was missing if there had, apparently, been so little to start with? Or had there been a lot to start with and she hadn't paid attention? She lazily fingered the beer mats before tossing them aside, picking up a cloth and wiping the rings on the stove. She drifted into the living room carrying the nail clippers. Sitting in the recliner, she inspected her fingernails for chips, then flipped up the leg rest and looked at the ceiling. Fifteen minutes later she weighed herself on the bathroom scale before grazing the refrigerator for stale munchies.

She realized that she had returned to the apartment

with the intention of thinking about George, but all she had thought about was herself.

After another month, Louisa called the police again. The policeman selected to interview Louisa was tetchy at being assigned a missing person's case but his enthusiasm perked up when Louisa met him in the lobby to let him into George's apartment.

As the river was still frozen, it was too soon to check the annual crop of double-glazing salesmen that always surfaced in the spring thaw, victims of the on-going window wars. Nevertheless, the policeman suggested that they go to the mortuary at the Vieux Fort and eyeball some corpses, in the hope, Louisa suspected, that she might faint and require resuscitation.

Louisa glanced sideways at Officer Jean-Claude Mercier as they drove to the mortuary. He had a crew cut, a starched blue shirt, and a Ford Crowne Plaza customized into a Québécois patrol car. He harassed the rear-ends of vehicles with Ontario tags until they got out of his way. When Louisa had first locked gazes with him under the wedding cake molding of the entrance lobby of the former Canadian Pacific Telegraph building, she read his vision of their future in his greasy, gray eyes. They would move to Laval, buy a bungalow with a den, a wood chipper, and a ride-on lawnmower, propagate a crop of Ital-Franco-phones, and when he retired, drive down to Florida every winter towing a mobile home shaped like a silver bullet.

Despite being used to inspiring instant lust, Louisa still found it threatening, and preferred to be in the safety of a relationship. She decided it would be better for her to secure some temporary protection in exchange for a mild mauling rather than skitter and dodge like a wildebeest in a park full of lions. Surely George would understand that?

Louisa dusted off a jelly bean rooted from the bottom of her purse and offered it to the policeman. She wondered if other people saw their fate hurtling toward them like an express train, and whether, like her, they decided it would be easier to lie down and let it run right over them. When they arrived at Vieux Fort, Officer Mercier bounded out to open her door. She tried to avoid comparing his rambunctious mannerisms with George's quiet presence, but he rankled nevertheless.

Officer Mercier's crotch appeared to itch with the excitement of public service for he tinkered with it swiftly before folding his hands behind his back and following Louisa into the mortuary. In an atmosphere of disinfectant and the woody aftershave of the chief pathologist, he opened stainless steel drawers with the nonchalance of a gourmet chef looking for a wooden spoon. Louisa sensed him standing behind her, his shoulders and buttocks braced, as she examined one homicide victim after another. She knew he was fated for disappointed; she wasn't the fainting type.

Week after week, they went to the mortuary together, but George was never amongst the carcasses with skin the color and texture of corn fed chicken. George had never been important enough to rub out.

Louisa couldn't shake the feeling that George had not been slung in the river but buried in the Molson Center's foundation, despite the fact that construction had been completed for some time. Four Saturdays in a row she placed flowers at each of its corners, searching the stone for a hint of George.

Jean-Claude Mercier waited in his police car parked across the sidewalk, his breath steaming up the windows as he watched her bend over to twiddle with the bouquet. She knew he tolerated her attachment to this missing man because he was confident in both George's inconsequence and his own machismo. Afterwards, they headed to the Plateau Mont Royal for dinner.

"What a healthy appetite!" said Aunt Sophia.

"Oh, I do like a man with hobbies," said Mama Baldetti.

"A dangerous job, you have there Mr. Mercier," said Uncle Tony. "But an honorable profession, nevertheless."

Papa Baldetti couldn't say anything, struck dumb by the eloquent request for his daughter's hand, the stiletto-sharp creases of Jean-Claude's polyester pants squishing stray pellets of macaroni as he knelt on the Pollock-like spattered linoleum of the kitchen floor. Handcuffs, cell-phone, pager, firearm and mace bulged from his thighs, like a flotilla of canoes in his pockets.

"You sure have a lot to say, don't you?" said Louisa, as they drove back to live in George's apartment, siren wailing, pedestrians scattering like dice.

On the third month after George's disappearance, he began to defrost on the aerial. His extremities drooped first, a hint of color rising through the glaze, like a TV dinner.

The first of May was the official beginning of spring and all the citizens of Montréal spent that Sunday moving cotton clothes to the front of wardrobes and pushing wool to the back. Louisa starched Jean-Claude's work shirts while watching a documentary about fish farming on television. She ironed five shirts per week plus one extra, in case the Hell's Angels biker war flared over the weekend. The television reception had degraded in direct proportion to the improvement in the weather but she couldn't be bothered changing the channel and she had never found the remote.

Jean-Claude returned from shopping for nails at Canadian Tire and found her bent over the ironing board, triggering the usual consequences. He broke yet another trouser zip in his enthusiasm. Louisa gazed past the TV's fuzzy screen, out the window and over the rooftop of Notre Dame toward a horizon that appeared to jiggle, nauseatingly, up and down. With one hand she clenched the ironing board for stability, and switched the iron off for safety's sake with the other, while Jean-Claude harassed her rear end.

George plummeted by the window.

"George?" she said.

Jean-Claude growled with satisfaction. His eyes were closed. He saw nothing. He felt nothing—well, almost nothing—but the hammering of his heart.

Louisa's heart didn't hammer. It was broken. It crunched underfoot as she readjusted her clothes, left the apartment and went down in the elevator, to find what she had lost.

"Wow," said Jean-Claude, standing astride the corpse. "Bet he wins a Darwin."

Louisa stared at him. Jean-Claude changed tack, setting course for the safer waters of banal condolences.

"He fell straight from the arms of the angels," he said.

"But why would the angels let him fall?" Louisa said, tart, peeved, pregnant.

She whipped her cardigan off and plumped it under George's mangled, balaclaved head. In her imagination she could already see George's former friends circling toward them over the cobblestones of Rue Saint Francois Xavier, already beginning to exaggerate their relationships with the fallen man, already making up stories about his life that were not true.

# Eilean Bàn

THE CEMETERY CLUNG to a bluff under a sky the color of cheap paper. Between a solitary croft to the south and Flodigarry Hotel to the north, its graves tipped wildly over an arc of shingle beach. Should the earth tilt by one more degree, all the souls laid there to rest over centuries past would slither down under their blankets of soil to be reaped by the waiting surf. Battered evidence of human persistency—the croft's buckled vegetable frames, the listing yet still standing stones, the hotel's gale-tattered flag—appeared to perch above a cauldron, for beneath churned the waters of the Sound of Raasay, and behind rose the Quiraing, an ancient escarpment of elephant hide rock topped with a tablecloth of moss.

The cemetery could be seen from the large bay window of Flodigarry's overheated lounge, where radiators gurgled above polished oak skirting. Comfortable, mismatched furniture sprawled askew on wide, warped floorboards scattered with threadbare Turkish rugs. The garnet, sapphire, turquoise, and ruby motifs had faded unevenly over the years. Some patches retained the intensity of first bloom while others had wilted as though steeped too long in water. Flodigarry's owners never bothered to rotate the rugs and the sun's footsteps could be traced from table to chair to music stand—proof not only that the world tends not to end, but also there are days in Scotland when it doesn't rain. Mourners grazed back and forth over them now, for tea or something a little stronger.

Normally the lounge was strewn with a congenial mess of board games and newspapers, but the newspapers had been removed and the games stacked untidily in the nooks and crannies of the bookshelves. Monopoly, Cluedo, Mousetrap, Tiddlywinks, Go—the scraggy boxes jammed sideways over folded chequerboards and National Geographic magazines. The contents of the oak dresser drawer—odd playing cards, dice, broken plastic tokens, jigsaw pieces, pawns, and the silver backs of long-lost earrings—rattled when jolted by the squeeze near the drinks table. On the wall above hung a ragged map displaying the locations of clan land from days when such things mattered.

Helen sat alone in an armchair by the window. She wore a neat and serviceable black suit, the skirt too long to be sexy, too short to be fashionable. Her limbs were folded across one another, her face to the view, a view partially obscured by the rain, each drop of which charted its own course down the casement window, then paused, suspended for a moment, before falling onto the earth. Although separate from the hum of activity, Helen seemed, somehow, essential.

The funeral party had settled comfortably now. The silent awkwardness of the first moments had passed. Laughter broke out, because it was hard to think of Fiona Hamilton without remembering something funny she had said or done. Helen turned at the gaiety, feeling no offence, and revealed she may be younger than first suspected. Despite heavy gray hair, whitening at the roots and clipped neatly at her nape with a Celtic clasp, her eyes, gray, wide, and clear were set within a smooth complexion, barely touched by make-up and, unlike the ruddy skin of many others in the room, lightly tinted by sun, like the souvenir of a long ago summer.

Of course, Helen had known her mother would die. Thirty years in the insurance industry had allowed her to calculate with actuarial accuracy the risk associated with the condition, especially given her mother's age, sixty-eight, and her refusal to undergo treatment. If such a case had been referred to Helen in the course of her work, she would have dismissed it out of hand. Her desire to fight these impossible odds had been as stubborn as her mother's acceptance of them. Fiona Hamilton had faced her fate as she had faced the gales that ravaged her garden every winter, with a resignation devoid of bitterness.

"It's not the end of the world," she had said, although for Helen, that's precisely how it felt.

After giving their condolences, the other mourners had realized that Helen was happy, (or if not happy, contented), to be left alone with her thoughts. All the other mourners that was, except Jess Murdoch, who strode purposefully toward her now, through the clutter of furniture and folk, holding a cup and saucer aloft, before arriving with a thwack of cushions in the opposite armchair.

"I was wondering," Jess said, handing Helen the tea, "About the car."

Jess had been Fiona Hamilton's nearest neighbor, their small croft cottages separated by a fallow field infested with nettles. She still wore the khaki parka zipped up to her neck and the black headscarf double-knotted under her square chin that she had worn at the cemetery. Others had shed their outdoor clothes on arrival at Flodigarry, and everything hung in the lobby cloakroom—all squished together, two or three items on each hanger, above a bucket of broken umbrellas.

Helen warmed her hands on the china cup and watched the light change over Staffin Bay. She inhaled slightly against the odor of damp wood and ashy pot-pouri, aware of Jess, quivering and alert, like a sheep dog waiting for a signal.

"The Land Rover," Jess persisted.

Despite years of accumulated immunity, Helen was struck anew by Jess's tactlessness. Her feet hurt and she wanted to unzip her boots and prop her legs on the footstool but felt it would be inappropriate. Across the room, Caroline Burns, the manager of Portree's Co-Op, had no such qualms. She lounged on a sofa with her calves being affectionately jiggled up and down on her husband's lap. The hem of her black dress rolled back to reveal a shell pink slip. Ash from her cigarette flaked onto the rug.

"The Land Rover?" said Helen.

"Aye."

Fiona's battered Land Rover squatted by the side of the croft in the same dirt tracks it had inhabited for the last twenty years. Helen hadn't given it any thought; indeed never thought about it, except when Fiona had driven them into Portree and it transferred the smell of dogs and oil onto her clothes. Fiona hadn't kept dogs for many years, yet the hairs and stench were so deeply ingrained that it resembled a kennel on wheels. The Land Rover masqueraded as a wreck, yet its peeling bodywork of royal blue paint, although calloused with rust, camouflaged a well-maintained engine. Fiona's indifference to aesthetics was shared by most of the inhabitants of Skye where the climate made a nonsense of vanity.

The Reverend Baxter put a hand on her shoulder. "We have to go now, Helen," he said. "Jazz and I need to drop in on Mr. Logan. He's a bit poorly."

"Of course, of course," Helen stood up. She thanked him for leading a service that had recognized her mother's cynical opinion of organized religion while celebrating Fiona Hamilton's reverence for nature, malt whisky, and truth.

Jasmine Baxter, the Reverend's Indian wife, opened her arms—the first time that Helen had been offered such tangible comfort. She had focused on the organizational details of death while accepting the swift, chilly handshakes of others who appeared to fear she was contagious with it. Some commiserated that she was an only child, as though Fiona's failure to produce siblings, (because it was a failure, naturally, they tut-tutted and shook their heads over it), had forced Helen to carry an additional burden of grief. The implication was that grief came in fixed amounts and that if she'd had brothers and sisters, it could have been spread thin over all of them, like a small knob of butter stretched over too many rounds of toast. But surely, she thought, grief was like love, bottomless, infinite, multiplying. The more people who had known Fiona, the more grief there would be.

"I'm glad I was an only child," she had said, thankful all those unborn siblings had been spared their scraping of it. "And that Fiona was my mother."

Jasmine smelled like warm wine. Her rope of silk hair against Helen's cheek soothed like a pelt. Helen closed her eyes and saw again her tears glittering in perfect ovals on her mother's plastic tablecloth, saw again how her despair had dripped unchecked while Fiona filled the kettle, took milk from the fridge, collected teaspoons and a sugar bowl, and talked of burial plots and insurance policies with the brisk bluntness of someone planning a sudden, but extended, and most probably boring, trip abroad. Finally, her mother, always impatient with sentimentality, had nudged Helen's elbows out of the way and wiped the surface dry before cupping a hand under Helen's chin.

"What's up with your face?" she said. "I'm no dead yet. Save your keening for someone who needs it." Fiona Hamilton had felt she'd had a good run at it, as though life was a high wall that one launched oneself against and either got over or not.

"So, would you be interested in selling it?"

"Take it, Jess" said Helen into Jasmine's hair. "Just take the damn car."

Reverend Baxter hooked Jess gently by the collar, and propelled her across the lounge. Jasmine released Helen, smiled, and followed him. Helen sank back down into the armchair, unzipped her boots and placed her feet on the footstool. She sensed holes in her stockings but she couldn't be bothered to check. Voices reached her from the room. People were passing verdicts, as, Helen thought, people tend to do.

"She hadn't a chance," someone said.

"True, true."

"The big C."

"It's like an epidemic in this country."

"Rampant, is what it is."

"Mind you, it was a lovely service."

"Bit odd."

"Nice wee change, though."

"Unusual."

"Why?"

"Well, I don't know."

"Do you check your own, then?"

"Check what?"

"You know, for lumps and bumps?"

"Oh, my Finley does that for me, isn't that right, love?"

"That I do. And I'd happily squeeze any lady that asks me."

"Cheeky sod."

"Got to laugh, haven't you?"

Around the room a string of names unwound, of grandmothers or sisters, daughters or aunts, nieces or cousins, who'd had this disease knotted under their breastbones, like competitors in some great tug of death. Helen sipped her tea, lukewarm and too sweet. She shuddered and replaced the cup, catching the eye of an old man with an unkempt white beard who glanced quickly away.

He huddled, along with three women and another man, around a coffee table in high backed chairs. She recognized them as the small group who had left during the service, dismayed, she imagined, by its secular bent. But apparently the Twain and the anecdotes, the Rabbie

Burns and the lack of hymns, had not stopped them from coming back for the victuals. Helen had no idea who they were and suspected that neither would her mother. Free Kirk folk, probably, from the remoter parts of the island, floating mourners who enjoyed a good funeral and felt justified to attend as many as they could, the kind of Christians who follow death the way others follow football teams and gleefully misdirect tourists on Sundays on the justification that hiking on the Sabbath is an affront. They discussed the funeral in urgent, audible whispers while devouring the smoked salmon of the sinner's family.

Most of her mother's friends had been Catholic because she'd said they were happier than the rest of us. They'd struck some deal, Fiona had believed, whereby they could sin all week in exchange for an apology on Sunday. Protestants on the other hand, like Helen's Methodist family, like these fundamental interlopers, were doomed to misery from the day they were born and accumulated sin like stones in a river, till they arrived at Judgment Day, buckled over, full-bouldered with it. Helen felt an urge to confront them for intruding but suspected that her mother would have told her to leave them be. Fiona had always enjoyed watching human nature pave its own path to hell.

"Poetry," one woman said. She said it in such a way that it sounded like an expletive. Her pinched face lacked eyebrows. She shook her head violently like a puppy over shoelaces before popping a whole oatcake in her mouth.

Oatcakes. Oatcakes, cheese, and tomatoes sitting untouched on a plate by the window on the day that Fiona had called Helen in Glasgow to tell her she had breast cancer.

"And anyway," Fiona had said. "It's no very big. Only about the size of a pea."

Helen had tucked the telephone under her chin and looked down into the back green behind her Glasgow tenement. Her neighbor was taking washing off the line with her daughter's help. With the corner of a blanket in each hand they heeled and toed toward each other like soldiers folding a flag over a coffin.

"What does Dr. Stewart say?" she said.

"Well, he's no pleased - but then," her mother chuckled, "It's hard to tell 'cause he always was a dour bugger."

"I'm coming home."

"What for?"

Helen had pressed the telephone against her heart and looked at the same sky she looked at now from Flodigarry, as though a sheet had been pulled over the world.

"She doesn't say much, does she?"

"Always were a right tight bunch – the Skye Hamiltons."

Helen recognized the Edinburgh drawl in these remarks. Karen and Cynthia, Helen's cousins had entered the lounge from the hall. The two women had probably been tussling over access to the small mirror in the ladies room. Noticing Helen in her niche by the window they drew themselves up sharply, like ladies-in-waiting halted by a large puddle. Helen let her gaze drift then glanced back.

"Mind you," Cynthia whispered, articulating so conscientiously that Helen could read her lips. "Fiona was the worst and I guess it's rubbed off."

Helen imagined they, like all of them, were sorry for her, sitting here alone, middle-aged, unmarried, childless. No one on Skye knew about her neatly managed life in Glasgow, her stylish flat, her convenient affair with an unhappily married man. She was not quite as drippy as they all thought. Not quite. And she longed to leave this island, to get back to the routine she had constructed for herself, plank by plank like a sturdy ark to sail high above the turbulent waters of living, and away from everything that reminded her of her mother.

"And did you see *those* flowers?" Jess Murdoch's voice rose over the rest of the racket in the room.

Jess could only be referring to one particular bouquet. Everyone had noticed it. On its initial sighting at the cemetery, Jess Murdoch had thrust her nose in the air and sniffed with satisfaction as though gossip had a perceptible odor. The brilliancy of the scarlet rosebuds, entwined into the shape of an enormous heart, against the brown-black soil, the emerald grass and the pearly sky had been as lurid, inappropriate and mesmerizing as a bloodstain. The bouquet's accompanying card read, cryptically, *"Together at last,"* and was signed, *"Isabella."* Helen had no idea who Isabella was. She would have to ask. She looked around for Moira, her mother's closest friend.

A fire blazed in the large sandstone hearth opposite a buxom sofa printed with peacocks and peonies. Moira sat at one end, her ankles neatly crossed, nursing a whisky and a box of tissues. Mrs. Stewart, the doctor's wife, had squeezed her comfortable roundness into the middle and balanced a plate of French fancy cakes on her stomach. Her legs were too short to reach the floor and pointed straight ahead like a child's. She looked like a tubby right angle.

Jess Murdoch sat at the other end. She had removed her Wellingtons, propped them against the fender and was wiggling her toes in well-darned socks before the fire. The parka had finally come off while the black headscarf had switched from mourning duty to napkin. Spread over Jess's arm of the sofa, it held a pile of potted veal sandwiches and a full round of petticoat shortbread.

Jess patted the empty chair beside them with a big, flat hand. Sitting in it might hinder a subsequent escape, so Helen perched on its arm. She looked at the three women in front of her and tried to avoid thinking about Macbeth.

"We were just talking, dear," said Jess, "About your mother."

Helen should have been surprised if they'd been talking of anything else but given the heated voices coming from the Smiths and Fergusons behind her, sheep prices were also much to be mourned. Moira sniffled a little and pulled a fresh tissue from the box, adding the spent one to the pile on the coffee table. Jess was obviously waiting for some encouragement, so Helen put her glass down on a tartan coaster and nodded.

"And we were wondering if your father would turn up, here, at the funeral."

"No, *you* were wondering Jess," Moira retorted.

"Do you mind him disappearing, Helen?" Jess asked.

Rory MacLeod's disappearance was news to Mrs. Stewart. She stopped chewing for a moment and shook her head.

"Sad," she said. It was the first time Helen had ever heard Mrs. Stewart speak. She regarded her with growing interest, wondering if any nouns or verbs would trot along to keep that adjective company; however Mrs. Stewart simply studied her plate.

"When was it now, Helen?" Jess's eyebrows wandered over her forehead in her effort to recall then she slapped herself on the face. "What am I saying? How would you know? You were too wee at the time." Jess stretched around Mrs. Stewart.

"When was it, Moira?"

Moira looked worried about the direction of the conversation. Helen smiled to reassure her because she knew exactly when her father had disappeared. She had been ten years old when she and her mother awoke one morning to find him gone, along with one of his skiffs, his fiddle, and some of his clothes. His wedding ring lay on the kitchen table. No note for his wife, no remembrance for his child.

Her mother had been bedridden for several days with the flu. When she pulled Helen into her arms on the settle she smelled musky from the percolated odors of menthol, toadies, and warm flannelette. Distressed yet, strangely, neither surprised nor worried, she spun a yarn about how Helen's father had rowed so far into the sea to meet his fishing fleet he was beyond the waves needed to bring him back again. The silkies would protect him, she said, referring to the mythical mermaids who visited the island in the form of seals.

"Do you mean he's dead?" Helen had asked abruptly.

"No." Her mother snapped. Her eyes had filled with tears. "No, he's not dead."

Since then, his desertion had been so rarely discussed between herself and her mother, or indeed between herself and anyone, that she welcomed any mention of him, thinking she could do so safely, without risk of repercussions. She had, simply, not allowed it to occur to her that he would appear at her mother's funeral, therefore his absence felt appropriate and unquestionable. In recent years she had considered the fact he may, indeed, be dead; however this proved too difficult to calibrate with the historical topography of her life that she had so carefully laid out for herself. At age ten she had pinned Rory MacLeod, firmly, on an imaginary map, in the shallows of Eilean Bàn, the island sitting mid-way on his row between Kyleakin and Lochalsh, roughly where the new Skye bridge now spanned. She saw him, mid-stroke in the larger of his two skiffs, with the waters stilled, solid and opaque as ice, and there he had, and would, she assumed, remain.

"Come on, now, Moira," Jess persisted. "When was it?"

"I don't know," Moira said.

"Ach, you do." Jess threw an arm in the air, scattering crumbs.

Helen picked up her glass to avoid contamination. "It was 1961," she said.

Moira flinched. "Aye, she's right."

"See?" Jess leaned back with satisfaction. "Our Moira's an elephant with the dates. I can never mind the year. I just know it was after that letter from Spain."

"What letter from Spain?" Helen put her glass down without drinking.

Jess seemed at a bit of a loss. Both Mrs. Stewart and Moira turned to face her, Moira having to lean around the considerable girth of Mrs. Stewart's set and blow dry.

"You see," Jess paused. "Fiona was a bit poorly with that flu that had floored half the folk on the island—I'll always mind it, it was like the plague—and there was a couple of days when I took her in some bread and milk and the post, to save her from having to stir from her bed." She took another sandwich from her pile.

"Kind," said Mrs. Stewart. She peeled the icing off her second cake with small incisive teeth.

Jess finished her sandwich in two bites and rubbed her hands together. "And anyway," she brushed the crumbs off her lap in a wide, sweeping motion, like a farmer sowing seed. Helen tipped forward from her perch on the arm of the chair. "I noticed this letter, and it had a funny postmark. It was the stamps that struck me, because, well, for a start there were lots of them and they weren't shaped like our stamps—more square—with a picture of a man with a big handlebar mustache—funny looking, you know?"

Jess scowled at the mirror above the fireplace as though the letter were reflected there.

"And it was unusual to get a foreign letter in those days—a letter mind," her finger stabbed at the ceiling, "not a postcard. And now too, come to think of it—it sticks in your memory. And I met your dad on my way out—he'd have been coming in from his shift—and I says to him that they were a right pair for the exotic correspondence." She laughed at her own joke.

"It was addressed to my dad, then?"

"Oh, no—it was for Fiona."

A small tremor rippled under Helen's historical topography. She slid from the arm of the chair into its seat.

"You know?" Jess picked up her final sandwich and chewed it slowly, shaking her head. "That must've been the last time I ever saw Rory MacLeod."

There was a short silence while everyone digested this information. Moira flexed her shoulders and finished her whisky. An ice cube banged against her teeth and dropped back down into the glass.

"Do you know what was in the letter?" she said.

"No, of course not!" Jess glared at her, indignant. "It was none of my business and I never asked."

Helen thought it was highly unlikely that Jess had never asked. She had asked but never received an answer. Moira slumped back in the sofa and sighed. Helen's palms began to tingle, and a familiar ache began lapping back and forth in her stomach, as though a plumb line swung from her breastbone.

She sensed it could be one of those letters, one of those letters that should never be lifted off the mat—the yellow telegram, the brown envelope with the portcullis stamp of Her Majesty's Revenue, the lavender scented missive addressed to your lover in handwriting other than your own—one of those paper Trojan horses that we persist on lifting and opening, allowing destruction to roar forth.

Still, this mysterious Spanish letter fascinated Helen, but she hesitated to pursue the subject publicly with Jess, whose passion for gossip often resulted in wild conjectures being pummeled toward nebulous conclusions, all conducted in stage whispers accompanied by much nudging and crumbs. Besides, Moira was obviously, and intriguingly, uncomfortable.

Jess stood up and stretched her arms above her head as though she was about to swing down and touch her toes.

"Right, that's me," she said. "I'm off—got to get home and feed our Willie."

She took her Wellingtons from the fender and pulled them on, tucking the ends of her trousers inside. Willie was Jess's husband, a man so rarely seen, Helen thought Staffin should market him as a myth and make a bob or two off the tourists.

"Helen," Jess folded the black headscarf over the remaining pieces of shortbread and put the bundle in her parka pocket, "You know where I am if you need me."

"Yes, Jess, I do. Thank you."

Jess left. Mrs. Stewart shuffled sideways into the vacant part of the sofa. "Tasty," she said, looking at her empty plate.

Moira stood up unsteadily. "I think I'll go and get myself something to drink," she said. She smoothed the front of her dress. The nylon crackled under her hand and the loose pleats clung to her legs like cellophane.

Helen excused herself to Mrs. Stewart and left her staring at the fire, possibly contemplating another adjective, her puffy feet still suspended in mid air. She followed Moira to the drinks table.

"Moira, I wanted to thank you again for all your help," she said. "You were such a good friend to my Mum."

"She was the best friend I ever had."

"Do you know who that bouquet was from?"

Moira handed her glass to the waiter. She pointed at a bottle of Tallisker without asking which bouquet Helen was referring to.

"Who did you call?"

"I just worked my way through Fiona's address book like you suggested." Moira took the refilled glass and frowned into it.

"So you phoned this Isabella, then? I know *I* didn't call her."

"I can't remember. I guess I must have." Moira looked, suddenly, very tipsy. "I can't believe she's gone—I can't." She swallowed the whisky, and Helen knew there was no point asking her anything else. "It's no fair." Moira gazed at the empty glass, her eyes awash. Helen hugged her, then left her leaning against the table, her hips dragging the cloth toward her in folds, and went to find someone to drive her home.

When Helen returned to her niche by the window, her mother's croft on the far side of the bay had materialized through the dissipating smur. The rain had stopped and the sky had cleared in horizontal streaks. It mirrored the flat lines of the waves and the treeless sweep of horizon. Everything was level now, even her mother, lying under the ground with her head against the Quiraing and her feet facing the sea as though waiting to walk on water.

Helen had often imagined her life, and the life of each of her parents, as a portolan, a map etched on a scroll of parchment, on which she had drawn the features and contours of their individual experiences with as much accuracy as she could muster, and with his or her name, (Helen, Fiona, Rory), elegantly scripted at the bottom right-hand corner, enclosed in a decorative cartouche. She carried all three portolans with her, grouped into a pilot, under her arm, so to speak. Over the years, she amended them, adding more detail, attempting to connect events, (known or surmised), within a superimposed grid of straight lines. This had caused some distortion, caused some things to appear of larger or smaller importance in proportion to one another, like the extreme Northern and Southern latitudes on a Mercator, than perhaps was truly helpful.

By laying each map on top of the others she hoped to chart a collective geography that, despite its imperfections and gaps, would ensure she avoided revisiting certain reefs—the disappearance of a parent, the declaration of an unrequited desire, the betrayal by a lover, the death of a loved one. Surely this was a safer way of navigating through life than relying on merely the sun and the stars?

The room was empty but for her. The sofas flattened as if by exhaustion, the carpet littered with pastry and cigarette ash. Everything appeared bereft. Could she really feel the earth splinter under her feet, as though she were straddling a fault line? She had always tried to chart her future course by mapping the routes of her past, but nothing had prepared her for her mother's death. No, nothing had prepared her for this.

She lifted herself, gingerly, and went to collect her coat. All the funeral cars had long gone, the drivers back to transporting fruit and vegetables for N.D. MacLeod, whose business prided itself on delivering whatever was needed on the island, whether it was food, furniture, corpses or brides.

It was not a long walk from Flodigarry round the bay. She stepped soundly through the drying puddles in the single-track road and paused in a passing place to let a string of motorbikes by. They headed toward Uig on the other side of the peninsular. She was glad she'd left some lights on at the croft. They beckoned to her with the promise of solitude. Solitude. She smiled at the irony. But it was unobserved solitude she craved. Or perhaps, unobserved mourning.

She kept her head down, watching her feet, glancing up now and then to acknowledge the small beeps of courtesy from passing cars before cutting across the beach, past her father's smaller, abandoned and rotting skiff. Inky waves lapped quietly onto purple shingles. Her mind emptied onto the stones and she allowed the waves to draw her thoughts out to sea. Her right hand curled around Isabella's card in her pocket.

The gate at the entrance to the croft lay open. She drew it closed behind her and secured it with the old rope. Turning toward the cottage, she paused because she thought she saw something move. Probably just a fox or a sheep. Then a light flickered briefly and disappeared. She frowned and squinted into the growing dusk. Pulling her hands from her pockets, she walked swiftly down the track, her heels slipping into the ruts in the mud. Close to the house, she made out the figure of someone near her mother's car.

She stopped and swore under her breath. The bonnet of Fiona's Land Rover was propped open, and Jess Murdoch leaned over the engine with a flashlight, her large corduroy backside thrust up in the air.

The Hamilton's had always called their house "the croft", even though it was no longer part of a functioning rented farm, merely built over the ruins of one that had been abandoned during the clearances two centuries before. Improved by succeeding generations, it had no stunted doorways or eroding mud walls, no lack of modern conveniences or thatching infested with mice. It turned its back to the only road on the peninsular and its best face to the sea, shaped like the houses children often draw, rectangular and symmetrical with a chimney propping up either end. Two windows bracketed the red front door, and another three pushed through the second floor wearing bonnets of blue-gray slate. On dull days its shingle walls, whitewashed every other year, made it appear to hover against the landscape like a gull.

The dominant inhabitant was the wind. It slithered through cracks in the casement windows and skirled around storing echoes. Thundering down the chimneys, it opened and slammed doors at will, forcing great breaths of peat from the fireplaces to heave through the rooms, causing everything to smell and taste of the earth. At night the croft didn't creak or groan, it whistled like a kettle. During the winters of her childhood, Helen had lain awake listening, believing the silkies had joined the bogeyman in the kitchen, to brew, endlessly, pots of tea.

Simply furnished, Spartan even, the rooms exuded old fashioned pragmatism, from the cream subway tiles in the bathroom to the knitted cozy with its brown pom-pom covering the silver embossed teapot on the kitchen stove. In the living room, a room naked of sprigs or stripes, of pretty ruffles or bric-a-brac, the hardy and plain hand-me-down furniture anchored rag-rugs tinted purple by mountain broom to the polished stone floor, forming barricades against the innumerable, cunning drafts.

Fiona Hamilton had never converted to duvets, but preferred her bed taut with flannelette sheets and itchy blankets. Her shelves, uncluttered by ornaments or memorabilia, held well-worn books, spines bent and stringy, filed in alphabetical order, the titles visible so everyone could see what she read; thrillers, biographies and horticulture.

Yet beyond those rooms accessible by Jess, the nosy neighbor, or the persistent, salivating evangelism of the Minister of the local Free Kirk, Fiona had attempted to restrain the burgeoning paraphernalia of her life. Behind attic and wardrobe doors, in drawers and under beds, she stifled boxes of photographs and old clothes, fishing tackle and a mangle, odd yardages of stoory fabrics, half-empty pots of white paint, a broken Singer sewing machine with scratched black and gold livery, a tapestry frame, crates filled with hanks of wool and spools of embroidery thread, wedding presents she disliked but had been fearful to get rid of on an island so small, and newspapers, newspapers saved from the Coronation, the Jubilee, and Princess Diana's marriage and death.

Obsessively, over the years, despite Helen's nagging, Fiona had kept everything—every chipped tumbler, every torn waterproof, every receipt, bill, and Church flyer. On the morning after the funeral, therefore, Helen stood in the kitchen, knowing, somewhere in this house, was the letter. If it could be found, read, and absorbed into her understanding of her mother's life without too much stir, (this she doubted, sensing it may, instead, radiate churn like a rock thrown into lagoon), then she could move on.

The wooden clothes pulley still dangled from the ceiling. Small seedlings planted in cracked china cups lined the window ledge. Tidy, frank, everything had little changed since her childhood. Her mother had never been secretive or unreliable. Indeed Fiona's honesty had been painful at times. But she'd also been too fond of human foibles to allow a friend with a romantic name and a taste for tacky floristry to go un-remarked. And Helen had inherited her mother's instinct for the missing.

She couldn't always surmise *what* was missing but she knew when it wasn't there. In parks she sensed an up-rooted plant from a flaw in the symmetry of the landscape. At restaurants, she silently mourned a forgotten ingredient. As a schoolgirl touring an art gallery in Inverness, she had yearned for a painting removed for restoration, drawn to its damp imprint on the scarlet wall to read the explanatory note, unreasonably annoyed. When younger, she'd often stalked ambiguities in other people's actions and conversations without the delicacy of discretion. Eventually she recognized the too human tendency to skip, suppress, and hide, and that the seemingly random pattern of life, like that of prime numbers, may never be understood. She recognized it, yes, but she never accepted it, and was ever alert to inconsistencies and gaps. She became wary of words and used them little, fearful what others may be conjecturing about her (because she conjectured about them) through what she didn't say.

Growing up on a misty isle, where mountains, churches, boats, and even her companions could appear and disappear in an instant, she knew that because something was omitted did not mean it was no longer there, it was merely veiled by haar, and always left a fingerprint, a shadow, a stutter. This gift of finding discordant keys, bitten back words, missing years, patterns in randomness—this gift of not stumbling and hurting herself on foggy days, was the only reason Helen had survived in an industry transformed by computers and the internet. Time and again when Caledonian Insurance wondered what to do with her, she astounded them by tugging at a suspect thread in a risky proposal causing another ruse to unravel before their eyes.

"Goodness, Miss Hamilton," the Chief Underwriter would say, torn between bafflement and annoyance, "that's another turn up for the books."

On the day following her father's desertion, her mother's characteristic practicality had temporarily faltered, so ten-year-old Helen took charge. She made sweet tea and refilled the hot water bottle over the sink to avoid scalding, just as she had been taught. When Fiona fell into a twitchy, sweaty doze, Helen tucked her pajamas into her Wellingtons, put on a duffel coat, and ran out of the croft, over the field, and down to the slothful slabs clogging the shoreline of the Minch, to look for Rory amongst the silkies. The seals' barely acknowledged her.

On her return, she paused in the kitchen doorway. Her mother, wrapped in a crochet blanket, was caressing Rory's wedding ring. Fiona slotted it into a worn groove of the kitchen table, and rolled it like a coin. It trundled off the edge, clattered on the flagstones, and skidded under the pantry door. Helen collected it later, rinsing it at the tap to remove dust from its journey and placed it in her mother's jewelry box. She hadn't wanted it to be lost, but neither, later, had she searched for her father when she became old enough to accept that he was not with the silkies but probably with some more palpable companion. To pursue him would have been disloyal to her mother, would imply that Fiona had not been enough for her and that Helen had needed more.

Her mother had loved her, this Helen knew. Not in the fashionable modern sense—there had been no "enabling" and "emoting", no attempt to be friends, fishing for feelings, or choosing lipstick together—but in an old-fashioned way with strictness about homework and bedtimes, swift dressings-down and cod-liver oil, with a short, sharp anger and an ever-ready willingness for mischief and laughter, with a black and white distinction between right and wrong, an awful tendency to speak her mind about Helen's actions combined with a feistiness for fighting her corner with or without knowing all the facts. Her mother had never told Helen she loved her. It had been unnecessary. Fiona would have been affronted to think anyone assumed otherwise.

I fed you, clothed you, schooled you, and sent you on your way, she would have said. There's always a bed here if you need it, but I'll no be offended if you never come back. What more did you want?

(For you not to die?)

And over the years, her mother's rare remarks about Rory had always been prefaced by saying that he was a decent man. A decent man, she said, decent, her tone reverent but resigned. What kind of decent man sails away from his wife and child? The kind, Helen concluded, who had done, or was faced with, something unforgivable. Skye was a community that believed in the fundamental inequality of men and women, therefore if Rory MacLeod abandoned his marriage, his desertion must necessarily have been the result of some deficiency in his wife. Her mother had never defended herself against the rumors that she was at fault. Why had Fiona, who had been so fond of truth and so laconic in expressing it, chosen to say nothing when Helen had known (for hadn't she witnessed it?) her parents devotion to one another? With the intuitive wisdom of a child she had recognized the difference between the homes of her friends and her own—known that Heather Malcolm's mealtimes were accompanied by a silence as taut as a mast-line, known that Mary McLaughlin's mother tended to walk into doors. Fiona and Rory Hamilton had had a happy marriage in a community awash with the usual reefs—early pregnancy, boredom, selfishness, alcoholism, unemployment, poverty, the stigma of divorce—a community of humans tethered to one another by habit and economics, like small craft in a busy harbor, knocking each other about—and they had fashioned their own unique kinship, sailed their own, singular, course.

Five years after Rory disappeared Fiona changed her surname from MacLeod back to her maiden name of Hamilton. Helen knew the gesture meant little. Her father was simply behind the haar, sheltering off the shoreline of Eilean Bàn.

Helen decided to tackle one room at a time, tidying or discarding the debris of the dead as she went. At midmorning, she took a cup of coffee into the front room and called the shop on Portree high street where Moira sold handicrafts.

"I wondered if you still had my mum's address book," Helen asked. She heard voices in the shop. There was a long pause. "Moira? Are you there?"

"Yes. Hang on a minute."

The receiver clunked down on a counter. Phone tucked under her chin, Helen wandered to the mantel to look at a photograph. In black and white, Helen, aged around six, clung to her mother near the ruins of Duntulm Castle on a gusty day. Her gingham dress had inflated in the wind like a parasol. Their heads arched toward each other like quotation marks, Fiona's fair, and Helen's chocolate dark.

"I was going to give it to you." Moira was back, whispering fiercely. "I just hadn't got around to it."

"There's no rush."

"I can bring it over tonight if it's that important."

"No, no, not at all. I'll collect it on my way back to Glasgow."

"Fine. Look, I've got to go."

Helen replaced the receiver, resisting a strong impulse to get in the car and drive to Portree immediately to collect the damn thing. She folded the photograph face down.

The mahogany sideboard was very ugly and very large, and it had housed the "Sunday Best" things for as long as Helen could remember. The doors and drawers had round knobs the size of tangerines and fronts carved with pomegranates and clusters of grapes. The whole mass stood on feet shaped like curling stones, like balls squished flat with weight, on a hideous Hamilton tartan carpet in the large, square lobby.

On the wall above were shadows from the brackets that had supported her father's fiddle, one of the few things Rory MacLeod had taken when he left. Her mother never rearranged the pictures of Highland cows to cover them up.

Fiona had kept bills and receipts along with every diary she'd ever written or discarded, and every letter she'd received or failed to send, in the drawers of the old mahogany sideboard. If the letter were anywhere, surely it would be here, and this, Helen realized with an itch on her palms, was why she'd left it till last.

She emptied the drawers, pulling out lace tablemats, crochet doilies, and the best cutlery, including fish knives with ivory handles yellowed to the color of old teeth. The last drawer held the papers she'd hunted through before, when looking for her mother's insurance policy. This time she examined each one more carefully; Fiona's wedding certificate, stained like nicotine with age and completed in a laborious calligraphy, the deed of the croft and a one-year passport.

A few years ago, Helen came across this passport when hunting for her own birth certificate. Until then she had assumed her mother had never been abroad. Fiona had been in the kitchen making shortbread for a Ne'er Day ceilidh when Helen asked her about the visit to France. Her mother looked up from her task with wide, bright eyes. She stared at the passport for a moment as though confused, before wiping her hands down the stomach of her overall.

"Would you look at that?" She took the passport from Helen and opened it gently, tilting it toward the light to examine the photograph.

"Helmet head." She bit her lip. "Used to take me yonks to do my hair—every night with kirbie grips and every morning with enough spray to freeze the surf." She handed it back to Helen and picked up a fistful of flour.

She told of her apprenticeship with a weaving factory in Glasgow due to her skills as a seamstress. In the autumn of 1950, before starting work, she'd been sent, along with other young women from the inner isles, to the southwest corner of France near the Spanish border for training in the chenille mills, a pointless exercise in retrospect, as the Scottish chenille industry had entered its spiraling decline. Nevertheless, at eighteen years old, she'd been as pleased as Punch with such an adventure. She never moved to Glasgow after her training, though, because Helen's father, Rory, had been mooching about Skye like a lost dog, driving everybody daft. She came home to put him out his misery by marrying him.

"It was a right hoot," she said. "Ten lassies let loose in France for six weeks." Obviously a tale worth the telling, but she said nothing further. She had returned to kneading the dough like a masseur over a particularly stubborn knot.

Helen flicked open the passport. In its small black and white snapshot, Fiona's hair was fair as milk. It capped her head in those kiss curls so fashionable in the early fifties. She appeared excitable, flighty, and laughed into the camera. The only customs stamp was from French immigration at Calais. Helen put the passport aside.

She finished her search more than an hour later. The letter wasn't there.

Disposing of perishables was Helen's last chore. She'd already packed her bag for Glasgow, and split her mother's papers into two crates—to keep and to throw. She took a sip from a glass of malt before emptying the pantry of preserves. Damson, strawberry, marmalade, and bramble—the date and flavor had been written on white labels in her mother's neat capital letters. The kitchen table full, she stacked the remainder on the draining board. They would make nice gifts for Fiona's friends.

Something bulged in the dark recess at the back of the pantry. She stuck in an arm, then whipped it out swiftly, thumping her knuckles against the door.

"Shit."

She had touched something that felt like skin. She waited until her heart-rate returned to normal and put her hand back into the darkness.

It was the jelly sieve, hanging over the edge of a stainless steel basin. Helen pulled the basin out into the middle of the floor. As large as a bucket but shaped like a cone, the sieve had a long strap handle like a trouser belt. Years of use had ringed the inside of the deerskin with a berry shadow that deepened to ruby-toned black toward the tip. Fiona had inherited it from her own mother, and believed that the more it was used, the better the results, as if flavor compounded with each subsequent batch, as if nature had a collective memory. Every August it had swung under the opened stepladder like a pendulum measuring the turn of the earth, and sweet, hot juice had dripped slowly into the basin underneath, the surrounding floor coated with newspapers. Sieving took days and was never rushed. Neighbors would leave empty jam jars at the back door knowing they would be returned full whenever Fiona made another batch. Months could pass without any jelly activity and then a delivery of quality fruit would arrive from the mainland and Caroline would call from the Co-Op, and every autumn Helen and her mother would pick brambles from the surrounding hills, risking wasp stings and nettles to get at the succulent berries, returning home with lips and fingers nipped and stained.

Helen pressed her face into the rough suede, overwhelmed by the sticky odor of late summer. She wept, rocking back and forth on her heels on the cold stone floor. Eventually, feeling drained and foolish, she wiped her eyes with kitchen towel. She could almost hear her mother. Are you quite done snottering over my jelly sieve? She folded it up ready to replace it.

There it was; at the bottom of the basin. An envelope with three square stamps showing the haughty profile of a man with a handlebar mustache. Helen stared at it for a moment, then lifted it out. She stood up stiffly, her legs cramped, and sat at the kitchen table. A knife had sliced the envelope cleanly along its top edge. It contained one sheet of paper.

There was a loud rap on the back door.

She held her breath. It could only be Jess. Jess knocked

at least twice yesterday but both times Helen hid under the staircase until she could sense the prowling Samaritan give up and squish her way back across the field. A second rap hit the door. Then silence but for rain pummeling the roof and windows. Whoever was out there would be soaked. She waited, her hand poised on the envelope.

Finally, an enormous definitive thud. Helen jumped up, her heart roaring, and stomped into the lobby and flung open the front door.

"Jeez-oh, Helen, you had me worried sick." Jess's hands were thrust deep into the pockets of her parka. Rainwater gushed off her hood like a downspout.

"Why?" Helen cocked her head to one side.

"You've not answered your door for two days!" Jess was indignant. "We could see your lights on and Willie was upset." Droplets dripped from the end of her nose and splashed on the doormat. "Go see that poor lassie's all right—he says to me—and here I am."

"I'm sorry. I'm fine," Helen tried to muster concern for Jess's sodden condition. "I'm absolutely fine. Come on in, you're soaked."

She opened the door wider, revealing the two crates of papers on the lobby floor. Jess's eyes sucked up the sight like straws.

"No, I won't come in." Jess looked down at her muddy boots with regret. "You're in the middle of something." She leaned so far over the doorstep that drips tickled the top papers of one crate as though the world had tipped on its axis. Helen swithered between insisting Jess enter or allowing Jess's curiosity to morph into pneumonia. She decided on the latter.

"Thanks for worrying about me," she said. "I'll pop over tomorrow before I leave." She started to close the door.

"Willie and I would be only too happy to help you clear out any bits and bobs that's left, you know." Jess's head peeked through the diminishing gap. "You only have to ask." The last toggle of her parka snapped free from the doorjamb.

Helen watched Jess waddle across the field from the front room window before going to sit on the stairs.

The single, heavy sheet of paper carried an embossed heading from the Ritz Hotel in Paris. Helen double-checked the postmark on the envelope. Segovia, Spain. She turned back to the letter. Although written in an elegant hand, the spaces between the words appeared larger than normal, as though the author had concentrated on each one deeply and separately. The text was very straight as if it had been placed over a lined template.

*Dear Miss Hamilton,*

*You will be surprised to get a letter from me. I am sorry it is so long before I write but we did not know where Juan was and I did not want to send bad news. It has been ten years and we could not find him.*

*No information comes from our government but that is normal. Last week I met a man who was held with him in the Fonollosa camp near Manresa. He told me Juan died there. He does not remember the date and will not tell me how he died. I think it not long after he came back to Spain. It was because of me, but I think you know that. He was arrested at the border. It is my fault.*

*I opened the letter you sent. I hope you understand, I thought it might tell me where he was. I keep it for you. I am glad you loved him. I am sorry for both of us.*

*May God bless you.*

It was signed simply with the initial "I", executed with considerable flourish. Helen flipped the paper over. Nothing on the back. There was no reason to assume, she told herself, unconvincingly, that this "I" had anything to do with the mysterious Isabella. She read it again, then placed it carefully on the stairs beside her, crushed by questions and scenarios regarding foreign countries and strange men and the coincidences of dates. The letter was postmoarked June 1961, the month and year that Rory disappeared, and it referred to a time ten years before. Ten years before her parents had married following Fiona's return from France. Helen had been an early baby, arriving but seven months after. Her mother had blushed scarlet when Helen had poked fun at her about this, wafting the birth certificate around a kitchen steamy with laundry. Fiona shrugged and muttered that such things were not uncommon in those days. Nobody minded as long as there was a wedding.

"And anyway," she had added slyly, "your father was a *very* attractive man."

Helen's father.

But her mother had spent time in France, not Spain. She wondered what that meant. And where was Manresa? And which government? And did any of it really matter? Fiona had gone and her secrets with her. Helen lifted her gaze from the hellish tartan carpet to the imprint left by the missing fiddle above the sideboard.

She stood up, readjusted the clasp in her hair, blew her nose, tightened the belt of her cardigan, pulling it and herself together, then returned to the kitchen and her glass of whisky. The Tallisker scorched a trail under her ribs.

Helen left for Glasgow early the following morning, and deposited the clothes at the Cancer Research shop on Portree high street before driving down the steep lane to the harbor. Moira's house stood at the end of a row of somber white cottages a few yards from the sea wall, the plain cottages that tourists turned their backs to in order to take pictures of the gaudier pink and blue homes of the King's Port. In the bay, a lifeboat bobbed at its mooring like a huge orange buoy. A rusty fishing boat idled at the dock, while another listed on the ashy beach revealing a barnacled hull.

"It's me, Moira," Helen said, as the door opened. Moira wore a snagged nylon dressing gown and soiledtoweling slippers. Her dull red hair had lost its curl. "Are you OK?"

"I'm fine," said Moira. "Come on in."

"I brought you a few things."

Helen gave her a small box, which Moira took through to the kitchen, Helen following behind her. Moira sat down at a table littered with crumbs, used hankies, and dirty dishes. She nudged an ashtray aside and began to look through the box.

"Oh, Helen," Moira drew a small string of pearls from a velvet pouch.

Helen told her that almost everything else still remained in the croft. "I left the keys with Jess—go and take anything else you'd like."

Moira fiddled with the remnants of Fiona's modest jewelry collection, placing each delicate pair of earrings in a row on top of the plastic tablecloth. With the last pair aligned, she lit a cigarette with a fluorescent green lighter. Seagulls circled outside, their laments insistent and harsh. Helen still stood at the kitchen door with her car keys in her hand. Moira took another drag then balanced the cigarette on a saucer.

"Want some coffee?" she said.

"Oh, no—I've got to get going." Moira made terrible coffee.

Orange waterproofs swung from a hook in the hall. The bulky nylon and rubber still carried the bearing of their former owner as though they were newly cast off. Moira's husband, a lifeboat man, had died a few years back in a failed rescue attempt off Raasay. She kept all his things exactly as he had left them. She propped the front door open with her backside and folded her arms.

"You have a safe trip," she said.

Helen looked across the bay. She'd hoped she wouldn't have had to ask. "Do you have the address book?"

"Oh, aye." Moira unfolded her arms and disappeared

upstairs. Helen caught the door as it started to swing shut. A moment later Moira returned and handed her the book without a glance.

Helen slipped into the car. She placed the book on the passenger seat and started the engine. Then she paused and looked at it. Her mother had used it for years - kept it in the sewing box beside the darning needles. Rectangular and thin like a chocolate bar, it had come free with some magazine that Fiona never bought again. Its laminated cover carried a print of a medieval tapestry of a lion and a unicorn. A fraying blue ribbon protruded from the top of the binding and acted as a bookmark. Helen tugged at it and the pages fell open at the letters "Q/R." She scanned down the names—nothing there. She would check quickly under "I." Just in case. No, no Isabella. She would have to start at the beginning and work her way through.

She looked up. Moira's lace curtain twitched at the kitchen window. Helen reversed the car along the jetty and headed up the hill to the town. The main square was quiet except for the usual queue waiting for the bus to Glasgow. The locals sat on benches reading the paper. Hikers with backpacks sprawled on the pavement. The address book could wait. Collecting it had been a mistake.

She stopped at the café next to the bank, one of the few open on Sundays. A tiny snippet of a place, barely bigger than a privy, it was dominated by a gargantuan Italian coffee machine. The one customer ahead of Helen wore a kilt, green socks and a khaki sweater with leather patches on the shoulders and elbows.

"Mocha this morning, Jeanie," he said, with a slight lisp. "And you better make it a decaf." He propped a walking stick against the counter, then frowned over Jeanie's shoulder as she poured.

"What's that face for, Mr. Campbell?" Jeanie said, appearing to sense his expression rather than see it. "It *is* fresh."

"It is the Ethiopian you're giving me, now?" He replied. "That Columbian stuff you had afore was an abomination."

"Would I lie to you?"

He took the coffee and paid, dropping the change in his sporran. A man entered as he left.

"Morning, Farquar."

"Morning, Ted."

"Shinty on Friday?"

"Aye."

Although she had been born here, Helen often felt like a stranger. Sometimes it was too much like bloody Brigadoon. She knew she would never be accepted as sgianagh, or native, by the locals such as this Farquar and Ted, not now she had left for the south. She asked for a small coffee in a large cup.

"I take it *you* can live with a Columbian," said Jeanie.

"I've never met a Columbian," said Helen, topping up the coffee with milk, "but I'd give a go."

Before reaching the Skye Bridge, she turned off the road and parked by Kyleakin's old ferry dock. Opening the book, she scanned all the entries starting at "A". Many were familiar and most had Skye prefixes. At "H" sat all the various Hamiltons—Karen had the most changes of number, for she moved house more often than other folk brushed their teeth, then on through "I," "J," "K," and "L." The letter "M" was extensive. A likely occurrence in a Scottish address book. It took a moment or two just to get through the MacLeods—James, Deirdre, Carol, Duncan and Cynthia and on and on—loads of them, not just her father's relatives but half the folk on the island as Skye was MacLeod Clan land. Then MacMillan, MacIntyre, MacKinsey, Marks and Spencer (Inverness), McCallan, Melville, Mendoza, Miller...

Mendoza. There it was. Isabella Mendoza. She flicked quickly through the rest of the book ending at Young's Butcher Shop in Portree, but found no other Isabella. This had to be it. No postal address, only a long telephone number starting with the prefix "thirty four," followed by "six" wrapped in brackets. She twisted around to look at the telephone box on the jetty outside the tatty Bonnie Prince Charlie Hotel. Inside it, two girls clutched the receiver and giggled. She turned the car engine off and waited. Trust her to find the only two teenagers in the entire country without mobile phones.

After ten minutes, she got out the car and leant against the door. A sharp wind sliced across the Sound. She was glad she'd decided to wear one of her father's old sweaters. Small bubbles of sea spray glistened teary on its cable knit. The girls noticed Helen and turned their backs. She looked at her watch. She should get a move on; it was a long drive home. Maybe five minutes more. She walked down to the harbor wall and looked across the loch to the mainland. Perhaps there would be no directory in the booth and this was a waste of time.

Clouds crowded the sun. The view changed from biscuit-box-lid perfection to sinister in an instant, as though an ugly thought had crossed the landscape's mind. Helen pushed her hands deeper into her pockets, and turned back to her car.

The telephone booth was empty. She walked briskly over and picked up the directory that swung at the end of a rusty chain and propped it between the coin box and her stomach. She flicked through pages spotted with doodles and ash until she found the international dialing codes.

Thirty-four. Spain.

The rest of the prefix must indicate the city. Wherever it was, it wasn't Madrid, Lisbon or Barcelona, the only cities listed. Surely Moira remembered calling Isabella, the one and only international telephone number in the whole address book? Those flowers didn't come to the funeral unbidden. But what did it matter? Helen had no intention of calling now, had she? Then again, it would take but a moment to check. She dialed the operator who told her that the prefix six denoted the city of Segovia, in Castile.

"Credit card details please, and I'll connect you."

"I'm sorry?"

"I need your credit card details before I connect you."

"Oh, no, no. That's all right. I don't want to make a call. I was just...you know."

Helen left the booth. She hesitated, then wandered onto the jetty. The waters lapped empty. The ferry no longer ran. In her imagination (influenced perhaps by tales of Norwegian longboats moored here hundreds of years before), this thin sliver of water between the isle and the mainland had buoyed up her father in his egg-blue skip. However this construct had conveniently ignored the Sleat's tidal currents, too treacherous for a single rower in a small boat, and that they had found Rory's skiff in the possession of an old family friend, to whom he had sold it, in preparation for leaving.

She could blame no one but herself for her predicament. Looking for the letter had been a risky enterprise, and yet she had looked, and when she found it (lying there, dormant, lethal, in the basin), she could have left it, yet she had insisted on picking it up and reading it, and the world felt no longer flat, but round.

The only sounds were doors slamming as men entered the Bonnie Prince Charlie for a lunch of bridies and ale, and the distant clipped zip of cars crossing the new, short, politically-troublesome bridge. The sky was clear, the morning haar dispersed. She stopped.

If she walked any further along this old jetty she would see Eilean Bàn, and its crisp shoreline might be empty of skiffs. With a little more common sense, and a little less imagination, she could turn around now, recalibrate her compass—adjust the terrain on the portolans to accommodate these new landmarks, these new inlets and gorges—into her known world where her mother smelled of the soil, and her father of the sea.

.